M000198175

Andreas didn't kⁱ up from his copy of t... _Zeitung_, and turn his head to glance through the dust motes of the smudged train window into the eerie morning light at the Bahnhof of St. Valentin. He was on his way from Melk Abbey to Dürnstein, a small town on the Danube River in the Wachau region of Lower Austria, a trip he'd made countless times, when he saw what he later referred to as "a vision."

At that moment, bathed in filtered sunshine, the beautiful woman lit up the shadowed station like the subject in a Vermeer painting in which the artist had captured the light and her profile to perfection.

Andreas did not have the soul of an artist. He tended to view the world in botanical terms. He compared his reaction to the way he felt when he saw his first tulip at the Keukenhof Gardens in Amsterdam—in full bloom, decked out in a myriad of colors, dripping with dew, bathed in sunshine. Exquisite. Now he knew how the frenetic buyers felt during the Tulip Craze in seventeenth-century Holland: He had to possess her. The breath caught in his throat. In that moment he knew his life was changed forever.

He certainly wasn't in the habit of acting on whims, and he wasn't given to spontaneity or flights of fancy. Like most botanists, Andreas was methodical by nature. _Nature_, ha, ha. Another botany joke that only his colleagues could fathom. Anyway, he didn't believe in fate, and he didn't have time for something as foolish and intangible as romance.

Praise for Marilyn Baron

"Marilyn Baron's *STUMBLE STONES* grabbed me from the start with its opening hook… *STUMBLE STONES*, named so for the plaques laid in tribute to victims of the Holocaust, possesses the best qualities of historical romance. Baron knows her settings and her history, and her characters, those both contemporary and in the past, are well-drawn and convincing. Baron has a great talent for dialogue, both in the banter of her modern lovers, as well as those engaged in much more serious conversations in the novel's past narrative."

~*Georgia Author of the Year Judge*

"*THE ALIBI* is an unfolding of a tale filled with Southern, small town mystery, intrigue, suspense, murder, and a bit of down home charm. [It] is humorous, shocking, downright scandalous in a small town sort of way, and an absolute enjoyable read."

~*Gabrielle Sally, The Romance Reviews (5 Stars)*

"Baron has a compelling and entertaining story that will leave readers craving more of these characters' lives! …a superb job with character development and credibility. As this mystery slowly unfolds, so many things are thrown at these characters in rapid succession—making the story fun and enticing! If you are a reader of mystery, suspense, and crime fiction, you may want to pick this up!"

~*Turning Another Page, Book Unleashed (5 Stars)*

"Marilyn Baron brings a unique style to her quirky and fast-paced stories that keeps readers turning pages."

~*New York Times Bestseller Dianna Love*

"A treasure trove of mystery and intrigue…."

~*Andrew Kirby*

To Cheryl,

The Saffron Conspiracy
A Novel

by

Marilyn Baron

Marilyn Baron

The Saffron Conspiracy
A Novel

Cover Art by *Debbie Taylor*

The Wild Rose Press, Inc.
PO Box 708
Adams Basin, NY 14410-0708
Visit us at www.thewildrosepress.com

Publishing History
First Champagne Rose Edition, 2018
Print ISBN 978-1-5092-2394-7
Digital ISBN 978-1-5092-2395-4

Published in the United States of America

Dedication

This book is dedicated to my daughters,
Marissa and Amanda,
who are as beautiful and precious as the saffron flower.

Prologue

Backe, backe Kuchen*

Backe, backe Kuchen,
Der Bäcker hat gerufen!
Wer will guten Kuchen backen,
der muss haben sieben Sachen,
Eier und Schmalz,
Zucker und Salz,
Milch und Mehl.
Safran macht den Kuchen gehl (gelb).
Schieb ihn in den Ofen 'rein!

Bake a cake, bake a cake,
The baker has called.
Whoever wants to bake a good cake,
must have seven things,
Eggs and lard,
Sugar and salt,
Milk and flour.
Saffron makes the cake yellow.
Push it into the oven.

Backe, backe Kuchen is a popular German children's song dating back to the 1840s. Saffron is an ingredient in many traditional cakes such as Gugelhupf, an Austrian Bundt cake.

Part One

O saffron flower! sitting in silent meditation.
~From a poem by Ghulam Ahmad Mahjoor

Chapter One

Bahnhof of St. Valentin, Austria

Saffron Fact: The history of saffron spans 4,000 years.

Andreas didn't know what possessed him to look up from his copy of the Austrian daily, *Neue Kronen Zeitung*, and turn his head to glance through the dust motes of the smudged train window into the eerie morning light at the Bahnhof of St. Valentin. He was on his way from Melk Abbey to Dürnstein, a small town on the Danube River in the Wachau region of Lower Austria, a trip he'd made countless times, when he saw what he later referred to as "a vision."

At that moment, bathed in filtered sunshine, the beautiful woman lit up the shadowed station like the subject in a Vermeer painting in which the artist had captured the light and her profile to perfection.

Andreas did not have the soul of an artist. He tended to view the world in botanical terms. He compared his reaction to the way he felt when he saw his first tulip at the Keukenhof Gardens in Amsterdam—in full bloom, decked out in a myriad of colors, dripping with dew, bathed in sunshine. Exquisite. Now he knew how the frenetic buyers felt during the Tulip Craze in seventeenth-century

1

Holland: He had to possess her. The breath caught in his throat. In that moment he knew his life was changed forever.

He certainly wasn't in the habit of acting on whims, and he wasn't given to spontaneity or flights of fancy. Like most botanists, Andreas was methodical by nature. *Nature*, ha, ha. Another botany joke that only his colleagues could fathom. Anyway, he didn't believe in fate, and he didn't have time for something as foolish and intangible as romance. Whether whim or will, he was compelled to get off the train, and when the locomotive sped away, and she turned, he was transported. Her beauty surpassed anything he had ever seen or studied on this earth.

She was no more than a slip of a girl, with long, straight, dark, burnished hair and a bow, for goodness' sake. The type of bow that might appear in the hair of a Catholic schoolgirl. It was a soft pink, embellished with a large woven initial "S," and the girl's creamy lips were painted to match. Her hair was swept up above the ears, and she wore the bow at a jaunty angle, clipped on the side of her head. He looked around for a mother or a nun or a companion—a duenna, perhaps—but she was quite alone. Who would have left that small beauty by herself, subject to predators and admirers alike, in this cavernous place some would say was the spookiest train station in Austria?

That day, a narrow arc of sun framed the girl's face so she appeared both angelic and naughty at the same time. She was deep in thought. What had placed that pensive Mona Lisa smile on her face? A lover? Andreas was already jealous, and he hadn't even met her. He hadn't thought of a woman that way in years. He'd spent so much time recently in the Baroque library with the Benedictine monks in silence, so many hours reading the manuscript and trying to crack the code, solve the centuries-old mystery, his eyes were swimming, and his head was throbbing. Now looking at this goddess-child, something else quite below his brain was throbbing, as well. Good to know his privates were still in working order.

Probably his judgment was clouded. He had been spinning conspiracy theories in his head ever since he started his quest, and he was closer than ever to uncovering the truth. A truth that, if he were right, would blow the lid off the Benedictine monastery.

The girl tilted her swanlike neck, looked over at him, and bit her lip in a crooked smile. *Erotischster,* certainly. But at the same time pure. And that gap between her teeth, so captivating. Her bow serenaded him like a siren's song. He turned away from the light that was burning his face. She must be staring at someone else. He looked around. No—there was no one else in the all-but-deserted station. She pierced him with her turquoise eyes.

Should he approach her? Was that too forward? Or should he walk away? The next train was coming in ten minutes, according to the schedule. Andreas always relied on a schedule. He found it comforting. Although, contrary to popular belief, Austrian trains didn't always run on time. He had only precious minutes to spare before the last train to Dürnstein. And he had an appointment there he couldn't miss. After his business was settled, he had to return to the Melk Abbey library, maybe for the last time, to confront the past.

The girl was still staring at him. Maybe she was

lost. He could close the space between them and see if she needed assistance. Contradicting his first impression of her as a child, he could now see she was fully developed under a clingy pearl sweater set. He was so excited, he had the urge to adjust his pants, but she was still staring at him. If he didn't make his exit soon, he was going to come right there in the *verdammt* train station.

He felt a choking sensation. Then he felt flushed. He wiped his brow. To use a favorite phrase of his British colleagues, he was standing there like a bleeding gawker. *Make a move! Don't be a horse's ass. She'll think you're a pervert.* He was paralyzed, her captive. But, miraculously, she made the first move, waltzing over to him as if in a dream.

"Excuse me, but do you know when the next train to Dürnstein will arrive?"

Andreas blew out a breath. Naturally, she had the voice of an angel, too.

"Dürnstein?"

Was he a parrot? He couldn't manage to speak a proper sentence, except to regurgitate what she had just said. And who was *she*? He didn't even have her name.

She laughed, and he heard a bubbling spring.

"Yes. You were on the train to Dürnstein, and then you got off."

"Yes."

"Do you know when the next one runs? I need to get to Dürnstein today."

"That's where I'm going," he managed.

She crinkled her nose. "Then why did you get off the train?"

He shrugged and smiled. "I honestly don't know."

"I've never been to the Wachau."

"What brings you to Dürnstein?" *Certainly not scintillating conversation.* Most likely she was a tourist.

"The wine, of course."

His shoulders fell and his face sagged. Of course. That was the typical answer. One day, if he had his way, the answer would be, "For the saffron, silly."

"And what business do you have there?" she inquired.

"I'm going there for the saffron."

She laughed. "*Backe, backe Kuchen…Safran macht den Kuchen gehl.*"

"Yes, but it's more than that," he said in earnest. It was important that she understand.

"Are you a chef?" she speculated. "Looking for ingredients for a creamy risotto?"

He should stop while he was ahead. If she discovered how passionate he was about saffron, she would surely run away screaming in boredom, like all the other girls he had dated. Saffron was more than a spice, more than a nursery rhyme, known by every German child, which lists saffron as a yellowing ingredient for Gugelhupf cake. Saffron was not just for risotto or paella. Saffron gave the traditional Viennese beef broth the Midas Touch. How many times did he have to spell that out to the pedestrian and the uninformed?

Mesmerized by her eyes, all thoughts of saffron, the spice that had fascinated him since forever, flew out of his head. Now that he had somehow captured this butterfly's attention, he couldn't let her go. Would never let her go. She had forever imprinted herself on his soul. He had found his mate. Literally. He was going to spend the rest of his life with this girl. She was surely his destiny. He was as certain of that as he was of taking his next breath. Apparently, all reason had vanished, deserting him in his time of need and leaving him with a primal hunger.

Andreas did his best to assemble the thoughts in his addled brain. "You're going for the wine, you said?"

"Yes, my uncle owns a vineyard."

"Who's your uncle? Maybe I know him."

"Malcolm."

"Not Malcolm Sutherland, owner of the Kleppinger Vineyards, surely."

She nodded her assent.

"I've been trying to meet with *Herr* Sutherland. Again. He wouldn't take the meeting and neither would any of the other Vinea Wachau vintners. They've locked me out. They're quite nasty, really."

The girl looked puzzled. "But Uncle Malcolm is really sweet."

"Apparently your *sweet* Uncle Malcolm and the rest of his friends are threatened by me. All I need is a little land. Where you can grow wine you can grow saffron. Some of his terraces are centuries old and no longer productive. They're covered over with scrub. It's land that lies fallow. Land he can no longer use to grow grapes. Land I was willing to pay a fair price for. I could grow saffron there and bring the terraces back into use. Your *sweet* Uncle Malcolm is trying to run me out of town. A town that has only nine hundred people. And when I went to rent a room at the local bed and breakfast, there was no room at the inn. It's not as if they don't have room for one more. They just don't have room for me."

"Perhaps you're being paranoid," she teased.

"It's not paranoia when everyone is out to get you," Andreas stated flatly.

The girl covered her mouth with her hand and stifled a giggle. He'd been told he had no sense of humor by his mother, his sisters, and a long line of women. Apparently, it wasn't true. This girl found him funny. But he took saffron seriously. It was no laughing matter.

"Every year, one-point-two million tourists come to Dürnstein to bike, wander around, look at castles, enjoy the landscape, and visit the vineyards, and many of them arrive on river cruises along the Danube. Surely, your uncle could spare a few of those tourists to a start-up saffron producer. I have big ideas, big dreams. Dreams that could help energize the town."

She laughed outright. Was she laughing with him or at him?

He grimaced, attempting to rein in his emotions. "You think this is funny?"

"No. Why don't you grow your saffron somewhere else? Dürnstein is just a speck on a map."

"It has to be there," Andreas said, balling his fingers into a fist. "According to legend, a knight came along the Danube and brought the first saffron bulbs to Austria on a pilgrimage in the year twelve hundred."

"Perhaps it is just that, a legend."

"It is more than a legend, *Fräulein*," Andreas said intensely. "You are probably already aware the town is known for its vineyards and for its apricots. They have apricot everything there—liquors, pastries, jams, creams, soaps, shampoos, even ice cream. But it's also famous for the castle above the town, where Richard

7

the Lionheart was held prisoner in eleven ninety-two. You can see the castle ruins from almost everywhere in the town. And I am hoping it will become known for its revival of saffron. I have everything tied up in this project. I'm determined to make a go of it."

"You're very passionate about saffron, Herr—"

"Bauer. Andreas Bauer. And may I know your name, Fräulein? What does the S on the bow stand for?" *Sexy? Studious? Scintillating?*

"It's Savannah."

"Like in Africa?"

"No, like the city in Georgia."

"So you're American?"

"I'm from Charleston, but it's a long story."

The locomotive chugged into the station, belching steam.

"Let me help you onto the train. Then you can tell me all about it." Andreas lifted the Fräulein's suitcase and helped her carry it up the steps. He had a sudden urge to know everything about her. To protect her, at all costs. To be her champion.

"Tell me, Herr Bauer, are you as passionate about other things as you are about saffron?"

Andreas blushed. "I think you're teasing me now."

"Maybe I am," she admitted. "Don't you think it's romantic that we met in St. Valentin's station?"

Andreas shrugged and looked around. "Romantic? Hardly. It's a train station."

The girl's eyes looked dreamy.

"Let's board. We don't want to miss the train," he said.

She placed a hand on his arm, and he felt an electric current. "Wait. I'm in first class."

Frowning, he pulled back the bag and walked toward the front of the train. "I'll just drop off your luggage in your cabin and walk to the back."

"No," she said, "I'm sure there's plenty of room. I'll sit with you. You can tell me all about your love affair with saffron."

Chapter Two

Saffron Fact: The cultivation of saffron in Lower Austria—Crocus Austriacus—is documented from the end of the 12th century until the 19th century. It appears to have arrived with the Crusader Walther von Merkenstein, who brought the seedlings from the Orient to Austria.

Andreas and Savannah settled into two second-class leather coach seats across from each other.

He tried not to stare at the girl sitting before him, but in typical scientific fashion he was observing her, trying to classify her, calculate her background. From her accent, and the little she had revealed about herself, she was clearly American and Southern.

"So you're from Charleston, South Carolina?"

"I was born in Charleston, but my father lives in Scotland."

"How did Savannah from Charleston end up in Scotland?"

"My mother was from Charleston and she met my father on a summer trip abroad right after she graduated college. But the marriage didn't last very long. Scotland was too cold and too rainy and too quiet for her taste. So they got divorced, and I live in America with her. I go to Scotland to live with my father every summer. He works for the Glenn Castle Inn on Loch Lomond, near

Glasgow.

"O ye'll tak' the high road, and I'll tak' the low road, And I'll be in Scotland a'fore ye, But me and my true love will never meet again, On the bonnie, bonnie banks o' Loch Lomond."

Where had that blasted song come from? Probably something his mother sang to him. His mother was very unscientific, ruled completely by her emotions. Prone to breaking out in song at every odd moment. And reading racy romance novels whenever his father's back was turned.

"Exactly. It's verra verra romantic." Savannah affected a heavy Scottish brogue.

"And verra verra pricey, so I've heard."

"Have you ever been to Scotland, Herr Bauer?"

"Please, call me Andreas."

"Andreas, then."

"Only to Edinburgh to attend a conference. And how about you, Miss Savannah. Is Scotland too cold for your blood?"

"Not at all. I love Scotland in all seasons. Scotland is in my blood. Loch Lomond is the most beautiful place on earth. The scenery is enchanting. When I first saw the place, I stayed up half the night just staring out over the lake, watching the moonlight glitter over the surface like diamonds. I'll miss the lake, but I'm looking forward to seeing the Danube. I'm going to get married at the Glenn Castle Inn."

Andreas looked alarmed. "You're engaged?"

Savannah laughed. "Not yet. Well, I mean, I was engaged back in America but not anymore. When I do get married, it will be at the Glenn Castle Inn."

"Are there any fierce Scottish Highlanders I need

to do battle with for your affections?"

"Not at the moment," she confirmed.

"Good to know." Now he could breathe. He sat back in his seat. "Why Glenn Castle Inn?"

"I've watched hundreds of brides walk down the aisle there with the Highland piper behind them and the ceremonial sword ahead of them, entering the elegant banquet hall. Here, let me show you."

Savannah opened her handbag and pulled out a faded picture of a giant of a man in a kilt and a beautiful woman in a white wedding dress standing in front of what looked like a castle. The woman was glowing and obviously in love.

"These are my parents. They couldn't afford a fancy wedding, but my father worked at the Inn even then, so the management pulled out all the stops to help them celebrate like royalty."

"Very nice. You look a lot like your mother. This could be a picture of you."

"Thank you. My mother is the beautiful one. Everyone thinks so."

Andreas thought everyone must be blind if they couldn't recognize this girl's exceptional beauty.

"So tell me more about this wedding of yours."

We'll be arriving by seaplane, of course."

"You and your phantom groom?"

"You can scoff all you want, but I've been dreaming of my wedding day since I was a little girl."

She was no more than a girl still, he thought. "And what brings you to the Wachau, besides wine?"

"My father recently remarried, and he and my stepmother are on their honeymoon. I think they want to be alone, so my father's brother agreed to take me for the summer. I'm going to learn the wine business and help with the planting and picking of the grapes."

Andreas raised his eyebrows. "Your Uncle Malcolm."

"Yes."

"So where did a Southern Scots lass learn *Backe, backe Kuchen*?"

"From my Uncle Malcolm. He says repeating nursery rhymes is the best way to learn German. But we were talking about saffron."

"Believe me, you don't want to hear about saffron. I could go on and on."

"No, really, I'm interested. I want to hear more."

"Seriously?"

"You must think I'm shallow."

"No, I think—the truth is, I can't think at all when I'm around you."

Andreas was happy to oblige. Saffron, a spice derived from the dried stigmas of the saffron crocus—*crocus sativus*—was his favorite topic. Wars were fought over it. People were burned alive for it. Kings and queens bathed in it. It had medicinal powers scientists had yet to discover. Throughout history, it had remained the world's most expensive spice. But where to begin?

"Saffron originated on the island of Crete, in Greece, but was probably first cultivated in or near Persia," said Andreas.

"Interesting."

She didn't appear that interested, but caught up in the history, he persisted.

"The Romans probably carried it to Asia. We think it was reintroduced in Europe from Southern Spain and the Middle East by the crusaders, pilgrims, merchants, and knights. Did you know that in the Middle Ages the punishment for altering saffron with other substances was being buried, and sometimes burnt, alive?"

Savannah drew back. "A crime punishable by death? Over a spice? That's barbaric."

"Saffron is a very rare and valuable spice," Andreas explained. "It costs roughly five thousand dollars a pound. In fact, it costs much more than its weight in gold."

"That's ridiculous. I don't understand why it's so expensive."

"You would if you knew how difficult it is to harvest," Andreas explained. "Seventy-two thousand flowers are needed to make one pound of saffron. I need to start planting soon, or I won't get a harvest this year."

"My uncle says the grape harvest takes place in the fall."

"Exactly. I'm running out of time."

Savannah coughed, hiding her mouth underneath her hand.

Ignoring the signs he might be boring his companion, Andreas continued spouting off the health benefits of saffron. "Egyptian healers used saffron as a treatment for gastrointestinal ailments and urinary tract conditions."

Savannah sat up in her seat. That was a good sign. He'd shocked her, but he hadn't put her to sleep, yet. Was he getting too personal? He couldn't stop now. He didn't want to overwhelm her, but he had to make her understand how important saffron was to him before she got off the train and he lost her, maybe forever.

"Saffron is the stuff of myths and legends."

"What is so special about saffron?" Savannah wondered.

"Saffron has a fascinating history," said Andreas.

"I'm sure." Savannah stifled a yawn. Her head nodded and fell forward.

Andreas blew out a breath. Dammit, he'd put another woman to sleep with his *fascinating* commentary about saffron. He recalled his mother's admonition, "Andreas, your saffron babble could put sheep to sleep."

Andreas smiled. He liked watching Savannah sleep. He imagined what it might be like to be sleeping next to her, to wake up with her naked body nestled in his arms.

Suddenly, the train pulled in to a station, and Savannah bolted upright.

"Are we there yet?"

"No. You fell asleep. I was boring you."

"No, you weren't. I'm just tired. It was the movement of the train. I always fall asleep on trains, and sometimes in cars, and sometimes just sitting on a couch. I'd like to hear more about you."

"There's not much to tell."

"How did you become a saffron farmer?"

"That's a long story," Andreas said, smiling. He hoisted his briefcase onto his lap and opened it. "Are you hungry?"

"I'm always hungry. I have a big appetite."

Andreas tamped down his unhealthy thoughts. "I happen to be carrying some of the saffron products I've manufactured. I plan to open up a shop in Dürnstein. I've already negotiated with some of the river cruise lines that stop in town to offer an exclusive saffron workshop along with a village stroll and possibly a trip to the Melk Abbey for a visit to the library there. I'm looking for space to live and to have a classroom to give my lectures, operate a show garden, and sell my products. I'm also going to sell starter packets so gardeners can plant the saffron flowers at home.

"Here, try this chocolate bar infused with saffron." Andreas handed Savannah a small, wrapped chocolate bar.

"Chocolate?"

"Yes, saffron can be used in making many products, such as chocolate, saffron-flavored honey, saffron vinegar, saffron sea salt, saffron almond liquor, saffron apricot jam, even saffron pasta. And, of course, the traditional Gugelhupf cake. I plan to sell them all over the counter at my farm shop and make them with raw materials from the local area. The climate in Dürnstein is ideal, and the threads harvested from the saffron crocus will be especially aromatic. As before, it will be one of the best and purest saffrons available in Europe."

Savannah tasted the chocolate and almost swooned. "Mmm, delicious."

"Describe the taste."

Savannah crinkled her nose. "A bit bitter, slightly metallic? It smells a little like hay. But I like it."

"That's right, exactly. You have a good nose." Andreas punctuated his remark with an intimate tap on Savannah's nose. "Saffron is very complex. It's not like pepper, which tastes hot or hotter. Some who have tasted it say it's dry, velvety, and dusty, and reminiscent of liquorice."

"What will you teach in this classroom of yours?"

"In my seminars, I will tell visitors from all over the world about the botany of the crocus, and educate them about the culture, how to spot fake saffron, how saffron is grown, and how to use saffron correctly in cooking. Then I will let them sample some of my products. That way they'll appreciate the taste and quality of real saffron."

"That sounds wonderful. And how do you spot fake saffron?"

"If you can smell it when you buy it, it's fake. The case it comes in must be airtight. Never buy powdered saffron in a tourist market. They will pass off anything from turmeric to brick dust as saffron. Safflower gives a nice yellow color and produces shaggy orange flowers and is often used as a cheap substitute. Unscrupulous traders buy a pound of safflower for fifteen British Pounds and sell it as saffron for twenty-five hundred British Pounds. Fake saffron could be soaked in honey, mixed with marigold petals, or kept in damp cellars, quick and cheap and adulterated. What's the first thing you think of when you think of saffron?"

"Rice," said Savannah.

Andreas's shoulders sagged. "Saffron has so much potential beyond rice and paella," Andreas argued. "It's similar to truffles in that way. You can use it selectively in desserts and other dishes. When we get to town, maybe we could go out to dinner one night, perhaps taste a dish made with saffron." Andreas focused on Savannah's eyes. He didn't have much time to seal the deal before they arrived in Dürnstein.

"Oh," said Savannah, twirling a strand of hair around her finger, glancing at Andreas's ring finger. "I would like that. Is there a Mrs. Bauer I should know about?"

"No," answered Andreas. "Only my mother. If you've never been to Dürnstein, I could take you on a tour."

"I'm sure my uncle will want to do that."

"Yes, of course, *sweet* Uncle Malcolm." Andreas frowned. "I've already explained to your uncle that I'm trying to rebuild the culture of organically certified saffron and products here so it will regain its importance and the quality it was once known for across Europe. I want the people to reconnect with this traditional product and understand its history in our local region. Eventually, I will introduce more producers. But I have to get my hands on the land before I can think about increasing the cultivation area."

"How do you know so much about saffron?"

"The Melk Abbey published a manual on the cultivation of saffron crocuses in seventeen ninety-seven."

"You've seen this book?"

"Yes, in fact there are actually two of them. And the modern monks knew nothing about them. One of them, dated seventeen seventy-six, confirms that four-point-five tons of saffron were traded that year. The other, written by a monk twenty-one years later, reports the decline of saffron production, and he wrote down all he knew about it. I've been researching the subject for the past year. It was once a thriving industry. And it will be again when I bring back the cultivation of saffron to Austria."

"Which you, no doubt singlehandedly, are going to

accomplish," she teased.

"Once I get my shop. On this trip, I'll be finalizing my search for the location for my farm and offices." Andreas wasn't confiding the whole truth. The truth was he'd already found a location. The perfect location. The location he'd discovered in the monk's saffron manual. The exact spot where once stood a thriving saffron farm.

"All of the products I manufacture will come with a story, and this story will be passed on to friends when they receive our products as gifts."

How much should he reveal about the progress he'd already made? "One day, I hope to cooperate with top chefs, perhaps partner with a Michelin-rated chef to open a restaurant in Dürnstein that offers menu items made with saffron. I've developed recipes using saffron for such things as saffron-infused sponge bundt cake studded with apricots, and crème brûlée."

"You're very ambitious."

"Just single-minded. In fact, there's a property I am looking at later today for my farm. It's an old railway station. It's not operating anymore, but the railway traverses the town, and it can bring people to my shop. It's only steps away from the Danube. Very convenient for my riverboat customers."

"What did you do before you decided to become a saffron farmer?"

"I was—I still am—an ecologist and botanist," answered Andreas. "I used to work with the EU commission in Brussels. But I became frustrated with the paperwork. I wanted to work in the fields. I wanted to plant. To grow. To work with my hands. What about you? What are you going to do with your life?"

"Uncle Malcolm wants me to learn the wine business from the ground up. He hopes I will want to stay in Dürnstein full-time. It actually works out well because I majored in Sustainability Studies at a university in Florida and I took some Sustainable Food and Organic and Sustainable Crop Production courses in the AG College."

"That's fascinating."

"Well, my mother doesn't think so. She thinks I should have majored in business so I could take over her company."

"But haven't you decided to live in Scotland?"

Savannah tilted her head and smiled shyly. "A girl can change her mind. You never know what tomorrow will bring."

"Why sustainability?"

"The world is changing. We're all global citizens, and we need to take responsibility for maintaining environmental health."

"I agree completely. That's why I will have one of the world's only bio-dynamically certified saffron crops. They'll be totally organic. We won't use chemicals."

The train slowed and pulled into the station.

Andreas pulled her bag from the rack above his head.

"I'll carry your bag for you." It reminded him of the idea of carrying school books for a girl in grade school. Did he ever do that? He couldn't remember. He'd never been exactly popular with the ladies.

"Thank you."

Savannah walked out of the railcar onto the sidewalk and looked around, taking in the Danube, the castle in the distance, the wine terraces and apricot orchards.

"It's beautiful."

"Where are you staying?"

"With my uncle."

A big, burly man approached and enfolded Savannah in his arms.

"*Liebchen*."

"Uncle Malcolm." She turned to Andreas.

"Uncle Malcolm, this is Andreas."

Andreas extended his hand in greeting.

Uncle Malcolm scowled. "It's you again. I thought we'd made ourselves clear. You're not wanted here."

"Uncle Malcolm! Andreas is a friend."

"Hmmph. Don't waste your time with Saffron Man. He has a one-track mind. And impossible dreams. Beware the dreamers."

"Is that Shakespeare?"

"No, that's Malcolm Sutherland. Let's go. Your Aunt Ilsa is waiting in the car. She's prepared a wonderful dinner."

Savannah turned toward Andreas. "Andreas…" she said plaintively.

"I know where to find you," Andreas assured and winked.

Savannah's face brightened. She leaned into Andreas and whispered, "Don't wait too long."

Chapter Three

Saffron Fact: Egyptian Queen Cleopatra used saffron as an aphrodisiac, bathing in saffron-infused mare's milk before seeing a suitor.

Andreas couldn't wait one more night to see Savannah again. He toyed with a forgettable dinner at a local tavern and nursed a refreshing Ottakringer Radler. The waitress was shapely and appealing, and she was even flirting with him, but she couldn't compare with Savannah. He couldn't get the girl's image out of his brain. Then and there he made up his mind. He was going to the Kleppinger estate right away to claim what was left of the evening with her. Herr Sutherland had no use for him, but he was Savannah's uncle, which left Andreas little choice but to confront the grizzly grape-growing gatekeeper.

He drove up to the entrance and parked his car on the circular driveway of the impressive Kleppinger mansion. A plump but pleasant-looking woman answered the door when he arrived.

"Can I help you?"

"Yes, I'm Andreas Bauer. I'm here to see Savannah."

The woman held out her hand and introduced herself as Savannah's Aunt Ilsa.

"It's a pleasure to meet you." Andreas shook her

hand.

"Thank you. You're the young man Savannah met on the train."

"Yes."

"Savannah can't stop talking about you. She's in the library with her uncle. Why don't you come in?"

"That's very kind," he said, running his hand over his hair.

"They're right in here." She gestured as she led Andreas into the lion's den.

"Andreas!" Savannah cried, jumping up from a chair by the fire to greet him.

Andreas smiled widely, until he noticed the scowl on Malcolm Sutherland's face and the tightness of his jaw.

"Harrumph."

"Uncle Malcolm, you remember my friend Andreas Bauer from the train?"

"Saffron Man," Malcolm snorted.

"Mal, please," Ilsa implored. "Don't be rude."

"Backe, backe Kuchen," Malcolm teased.

"Malcolm!" Ilsa warned.

"Pat-a-cake, pat-a-cake, baker's man. Bake me a cake as fast as you can."

"Now you're just being childish," Ilsa said.

"Ilsa, this man is not here to see our niece. He is here to pester me about my vineyards. He's using Savannah to get to me."

"That's not true," Andreas insisted.

"Is it not true that you want to purchase my land?"

"Your wine terraces are centuries old," Andreas pointed out. "They're no longer productive. I could bring the terraces back into use with local production of saffron, which will be organic and biodynamic. I'm willing to pay a fair price."

"Yes, I've heard your sales pitch before. Nobody is interested in your wild dreams of saffron, Baker Boy," Malcolm spit out. "Wine is the backbone of this region. It always has been. It always will be."

"That's why the Wachau vineyards are so perfect for growing saffron, with their dry soil and sunny climate," Andreas pointed out.

"We're attracting hundreds of tourists to our historic wine estate visits to sample our organic wines and drinkable vinegars. Tourists love the tastings and the fact that we're one of the oldest wineries in Austria and that we produce some of the world's best Rieslings."

"I've also made arrangements with the cruise lines to set up tours of my saffron operation."

"I think you're getting ahead of yourself. How many people do you think will be getting on the buses to come to your saffron farm, which, as I understand it, doesn't yet exist?"

"You're wrong, Herr Sutherland. I believe there will be a demand. You get busloads of people with each cruise stop. Surely you won't mind if a few elect to try a different excursion."

"Harrumph," Malcolm snorted again.

"I've found a place," Andreas announced. "There's a train running right by where my shop will be. It will take visitors around the town and stop at my model saffron garden."

Malcolm bellowed with laughter. "Ah, the old railway station…the train to nowhere."

"Uncle Malcolm, you should listen to Andreas.

He's an expert. He plans to revive saffron cultivation in the Wachau."

Malcolm sprang from the couch. "I've heard enough. If you want a man, I'll find you a good vintner from a respectable family. In fact, I have an excellent candidate in mind. He's the son of my good friend Rudolf, who owns the vineyard bordering our property. His son, Lukas, is about your age. He will inherit his father's vineyard one day. It would be quite a merger. He is very eligible. He can teach you a lot. Anyone can plainly see this fool you've gotten yourself mixed up with has no future."

"Uncle Malcolm!" Savannah admonished. She picked up her handbag and joined hands with Andreas in a show of support.

"I'm only looking out for your future. I've already arranged a meeting between you and young Lukas. I think you two will be very well-suited."

"Uncle Malcolm! It sounds like you're auctioning me off like a cow. I don't need you to find a man for me. I'm quite capable of finding one for myself, as you can plainly see."

"A man you picked up at a train station?" Malcolm laughed.

"I'm going out," she announced, stamping her foot like an angry bull.

"Where are you going?" Uncle Malcolm demanded.

"With Andreas."

"Hot tempered and stubborn, just like your mother," Malcolm whispered under his breath.

Savannah wore another bow in her hair, this time a violet silk clip-on, imprinted with her signature "S" and matching her creamy lipstick. Her sweater dress was clingy and showed plenty of curves, but at the same time, it was tasteful. The girl knew how to dress to accentuate her considerable assets. If he was lucky, he was going to get a taste of that lipstick later in the evening. And maybe a touch of the rest of her. Andreas felt her warmth as she clung to his arm.

"Uncle Malcolm, Aunt Ilsa, I'll see you later."

"Be sure to have my niece home at a decent hour and don't bore her to death with your saffron stories," Uncle Andreas barked. "My niece sees something in you, but I can't imagine what."

"Yes, sir," said Andreas, extending his hand. Malcolm ignored the gesture and turned his back to the couple as he walked over to the fireplace to stoke the fire.

"I apologize for Uncle Malcolm," Savannah said when they were out the door.

He helped Savannah into the passenger seat of his rental car.

"Your uncle hates me," he said as he started the engine.

"He doesn't know you."

"Neither do you, for that matter."

"I know enough. You are passionate about saffron. I like that."

Right now Andreas was feeling passionate about Savannah. There was an unseasonal chill in the air, and it didn't escape Andreas's notice that a hint of Savannah's nipples was on display through the form-fitting wool of her outfit.

"Where shall we go?" he asked. "Have you eaten?"

"Yes, my aunt fixed a big meal."

"How about an after-dinner drink, some wine, perhaps?"

From the glazed look in her eyes, Savannah had already had a great deal of wine for dinner. Of course. She was a vintner's niece. But apparently, she was a lightweight when it came to alcohol consumption. Promising.

"Do you have a place?"

"Yes," said Andreas. "A small bed and breakfast owned by someone who's not owned by your uncle."

"Take me there."

Andreas's hands shook on the wheel.

Savannah looked at him adoringly, her eyelids flagging.

"I'm not sure that's such a good idea. I think you've had too much to drink already."

Savannah sported a goofy smile. "Then where shall we go?"

"It's still light out. I want to show you something."

Savannah's bow slipped and threatened to fall from her satiny mane.

"Another bow?" Andreas asked as he slowed the car, cradled Savannah's head and fixed the bow back into place.

"My mother owns an accessories shop called Southern Signature Accessories. She sells bows, belts, T-shirts, hats, handbags, and other clothing items. I've been wearing bows in my hair since I was in grade school. My mother says it makes a fashion statement and it's good for business. She says a bow completes an ensemble, like gloves would put the finishing touch on an outfit in the past. Her motto is, 'Dress like you have nothing else on.' We sell the perfect bow for every occasion. Don't you like bows?"

"Very much," Andreas said. "Especially on you. And your initial, S, is on each bow?"

"Yes, my mother personalizes all the products at her shop. Where are you taking me?"

"I have a surprise for you."

Savannah clapped her hands. "Oh, I love surprises, Andreas."

She was still so much a child, but in a desirable woman's body, Andreas thought. A body he was eager to explore. But he had to rein in his impulses so as not to scare her away. After all, it was only their first date. Not even an official date. The specter of Uncle Malcolm's wrath was unsettling. And he was less than enthusiastic about the prospect of Savannah's potential suitor, Lukas.

He'd made a lot of progress since he left Savannah at the station. He'd signed the contract for the house on the old railroad route where he would live, locate his shop, conduct classes and perhaps hold special events for gourmets and hobby gardeners, and tend his modest saffron garden. The seller offered the railroad that ran in front of the house as part of the deal. A railroad hadn't been in his plans. But then he thought about how he had met Savannah and it seemed serendipitous. So he agreed.

There was enough room for Andreas, a wife, and at least two children. Now he just had to convince Savannah that his prospects were good. And he'd need to purchase some additional acres. That was a problem, since none of the vintners were excited about an outsider moving into their territory and supplanting them. Not an insurmountable obstacle, but problematic at this point.

Andreas drove to the bottom of the street, slowed the car, and pulled into the parking lot at the back of a two-story house. He went around to the passenger side and helped Savannah out of the car. She was a little unsteady on her feet. He turned her around to get her first glimpse of what he hoped would be their new home and placed his hands on her shoulders to steady her.

"What is this place, Andreas?"

"My new house. I picked up the key today."

Hand in hand, he walked Savannah around the property. Her hand felt good in his. Warm and solid. Like it belonged there. Just right.

"Do you like it? The master bedroom upstairs has a beautiful view of the Danube, from the balcony." He unlocked the door and led her from room to room. "It's very close to the river. That way when people get off the boat and take an excursion, I'll have them picked up and driven here for my lectures. Here's the lecture room. And next door is a nice space for a shop. Behind the shop, a large kitchen to manufacture the saffron products. And look here—a display garden. Of course we're going to need real fields eventually, but this is a start. People in town will see, and they will come to accept the saffron and me."

"Andreas, there's a train station in front of this house."

"This railway station is not in use, but it will be. Customers will come from all over the region and Austria to visit my shop."

"How will you arrange that?"

"I bought the station."

"You bought a train station?"

"Yes, an old railway station. It's perfect."

"We met at a train station," Savannah reminded him, smiling and crinkling her nose.

"Perhaps we were fated to meet," Andreas said, although he was a scientist and didn't much believe in unproven things, or even God. He believed in science. But as he stared into Savannah's sparkling eyes, he thought there might have been a divine hand in their chance meeting.

"What do you think of the house behind the station? There's room for a small family." Andreas took a chance. "Plenty of room for children," he whispered. "The house is in wonderful shape. All it needs is a woman's touch, I think." He squeezed Savannah's hand, and she didn't resist. She shivered.

"Are you cold?"

Savannah bit her lip. "Not cold, Andreas." She looked up at him.

"Do you want children?"

Savannah's fathomless green eyes widened. "Not anytime soon. Maybe, one day."

Andreas was on a more compressed timetable. He already imagined Savannah at home, playing with the children, helping in the garden and the shop. Making saffron products in the kitchen. Wearing nothing under her apron and nothing on her body but a bow. She would make a pretty picture and a pleasing wife.

"All organisms must propagate, by sexual or asexual reproduction," Andreas observed. "It's essential—the natural order of things."

"Are you talking about plants or people?"

"Well, both."

"Spoken like a true botanist."

"It's what I believe."

"When I need advice on breeding, I'll be sure to ask you."

"I didn't mean to be presumptuous."

"Well, we have all summer to talk about it. After that, I'll be gone. That's what I do. After the summer, I leave."

"Can you ever imagine yourself living in Dürnstein?"

Savannah hesitated. "I always thought I would live in Scotland."

"It's very lovely, and only an hour away from Vienna, where I'm from."

After they explored the kitchen, and the offices, they stood outside looking at the railroad tracks running by the house.

"Why are you showing me this house?"

Testing the waters, he said, "It could be ours."

Savannah raised her eyebrows and removed her hand from his. "It's a wonderful house, Andreas. I can see how a family could be very happy here. But—"

Andreas cleared his throat. Clearly, he was rushing her. Maybe he had imagined their connection. She wasn't ready to open up for him, yet. Plants needed tending and nurturing. So did relationships, before they could blossom, he thought. He was impatient, but he smothered his expectations. He was willing to put his dreams on hold. Savannah would be worth the wait.

"Yes. Well, then, look here, the railway will stop right in front of the shop. Can't you just imagine it? My sign will go here, here will be the model garden, and plenty of space for the classroom and the shop."

"Hmm." She leaned into him. "Sometimes you seem more fascinated with the saffron crocus than with me," Savannah quipped.

Was she warming to him? Or was she falling asleep? Apparently, the woman could fall asleep at the drop of a hat. Or maybe she was intoxicated. He certainly was, and he hadn't had more than a drop to drink.

Was her signal an invitation to proceed? He didn't have much experience with relationships. Plants were very responsive to his attentions. But women? Who knew?

Taking a chance, Andreas put his arms around Savannah's waist and pulled her close. "I think I will die if I don't kiss you."

He didn't wait for an answer. He covered her mouth with his as he inched closer.

She kissed him back. It was heaven. His hands moved involuntarily toward her breasts, but he hesitated. He tightened his hold on Savannah and deepened the kiss.

"Andreas," she said, breathless. "Take me."

"Take you where?"

"Take me."

"Oh. I think you've been reading too many romance novels. You have a passionate nature. The only place I'm going to take you is home, before we get carried away. Although I know I'm going to regret this in the morning." He was already starting to regret it.

Chapter Four

Saffron Fact: Alexander the Great and his forces are said to have used saffron during their Asian campaigns in their baths to heal battle wounds.

"I'm doing fine, Mama." Savannah spoke into her cell phone.

"Are you getting into any trouble?"

"No." Savannah crossed her fingers, although her mother couldn't see them.

"Maybe you should. All those boring nights in Scotland, you're probably ready to break out."

"I love Scotland. It's never boring."

"Speaking of boring men, how's your father?"

"I haven't heard from him since the honeymoon," Savannah reported.

"His new wife is probably wearing him out. What's her name again, Kiki? Suzi? Something with an "i" at the end."

"Cindi."

"She's half his age. I hope he doesn't have a heart attack in the honeymoon suite. I'm surprised she got him to leave that damned inn."

"Mother! Are you jealous?"

"Who, me? I have nothing to be jealous of. But your father will always have a special place in my heart. I hope she keeps him warm on those brutal

Scottish nights. Better her than me."

"It took him years to get over you. And when you deserted him you took me with you."

"He had you for the summers."

"He deserves a little happiness. And Cindi seems to make him happy."

"She's not good enough for him," Dina asserted.

"Maybe not. But she's there, which is more than you were."

Typical Dina. She wants what she can't have. She may not want Connor, but she doesn't want anyone else to have him. Savannah shook her head. She'd spent half her life trying to get her sparring parents back together until she realized she was the only common denominator in that relationship.

And then when Cindi with an "i" came along, Da was lovestruck, acting like a besotted schoolboy. Suddenly, he had tons of energy. He wanted to travel. Her mother hadn't had any luck getting him off that "damn island," as she called Scotland. But Cindi, with her model slender body, seemingly unencumbered by her ponderous breasts, crooked her little finger and Da came running.

At the wedding, everyone kept mistaking the groom for the father of the bride. Embarrassing, but she respected his choice so she bit her tongue and swallowed the fact that her new stepmother, a waitress in the restaurant at the inn, was closer to her age than his.

"So what are you up to? How are Malcolm and Ilsa?"

"They're fine."

"Did you know he hit on me at our wedding?"

"Mama!"

"It's true. You need to know what kind of man your uncle is."

"He's always been polite to me."

"Then he's on his best behavior. Just watch out. He usually gets what he wants."

Savannah rolled her eyes. Her mother had always been a bit of a drama queen. And at times, she could be outrageous.

"So tell me, what have you been up to?"

"Nothing. Uncle Malcolm is offering me up to one of his friend's sons."

"Offering you up? As a sacrifice?"

"Pretty much. There's another vintner with property next to his that Uncle Malcolm has been coveting, and he has visions of merging the two properties."

"Just what does this boy look like?"

"I haven't met him yet. Uncle Malcolm and Aunt Ilsa are planning a dinner party this evening. I'll meet him then, but, Mama, I've already met someone."

"You just got there."

"I met him at the train station."

"Is he a conductor?"

"No, Mother, he's a botanist. And he's going to become a saffron farmer."

"A saffron farmer? For heaven's sake. You're interested in another farmer, like Sullivan?"

"Sully was not a farmer. He was an onion broker."

"Whatever that is. I think Sullivan was just after your money."

"Mother, Sully had plenty of money of his own. He made a fortune in sweet onions."

"Didn't he tell you he wanted his ashes scattered over Vidalia or Peru or wherever he sources his onions?"

"No, Mother, he wanted to be frozen."

"Frozen? Promise me you're not going to spend your inheritance to freeze Sullivan."

"Don't worry. I broke off the engagement."

"I'm glad you saw the light before you married the man. Why did you break it off?"

"Sully wanted children and I didn't."

"Well, I'm too young to be a grandmother right now," Dina said. "But one day. I could start an infant hair bow line."

"Mother, a decision to have children should not be based on a business model. And I don't think I will ever have children."

"Why ever not?"

Savannah frowned. How could she explain to her mother the loneliness she'd felt growing up, the feeling she didn't belong in one place or another. A feeling she never wanted her children to have. She couldn't express these thoughts to her mother without laying blame. And what good would that do now?

"And now you're taking up with another farmer? Is he as good-looking as Sullivan?"

"Well, no. He's not your type. But I don't care how he looks. That's not important to me. I think he cares for me, and I like him too, very much. Although he speaks so lovingly about saffron, it's like he's talking about his mistress."

"There's nothing wrong with passion. And surely you can't be jealous of a plant. But what kind of name is Andreas?"

"He's Austrian, from Vienna."

"Don't make the same mistake I did. I fell for a pair of broad shoulders and a Scottish brogue. I was tempted to see if he wore anything under those kilts of his."

"Mother, don't be crude." Although she herself had been tempted to test that theory on the men she'd dated in Glasgow. "And he's not a Scot."

"Does he know how wealthy I am? He may be after your money, too."

"Why do you think every boy is after my money? How do you think that makes me feel?"

"I'm just saying you have to be careful. It's all part of the equation. Does he have any money of his own?"

"Well, I don't think he has much to his name. He thinks you run a little bow shop in Charleston."

"Ha! Let's hope he doesn't Google me and find my 'little bow shop' on the New York Stock Exchange. And while we're on the subject, do I need to remind you that I'm leaving all of my little bow shops to you? So don't get too comfortable in Austria."

"Uncle Malcolm has hinted that he might want me to stay in Dürnstein permanently. And Daddy wants me to stay in Scotland so he can keep me his little girl forever."

"That's exactly why I left your father and Scotland, because I *didn't* want a man to tell me where to live and how to live my life."

"Yet that's exactly what you're trying to do to me."

"Well, what is it you want to do with your life?"

"Something where I can use my major in Sustainability Studies."

"And what exactly do you intend to do with that

degree? It isn't exactly the path to fame and fortune."

"And has your fortune made you happy?"

"All your father wanted was a wife to keep him warm in his bed and raise babies. I don't want the same thing to happen to you. You're coming back to Charleston when the summer is over. It's time you took some responsibility."

"And what if I don't want to come back to Charleston? You know how much I love Scotland."

"I didn't work this hard to leave my company to a stranger. Savannah, what exactly are you looking for?"

"Love."

"Love doesn't exist, not forever anyway. Learn from my mistakes."

Savannah sighed, wondering if she was one of her mother's mistakes. "I have to go. I'm meeting Andreas later."

"I hope he's from a good family."

"I don't know anything about his family. I know him, and that's all I need to know."

"Well, don't say I didn't warn you, when you're down on your hands and knees picking saffron to make ends meet."

"Mother, I'm not going to marry him. And what do you think people do in a vineyard?"

"Your Uncle Malcolm is a very successful vintner. You can't compare the two."

"I'll remember that. I love you. Talk to you soon."

"Are you still wearing your bows?"

"Of course." Hopefully, her mother would never find out her bow was what first attracted Andreas to her. In fact, the other night he'd mentioned he'd like to see her dressed in nothing but a bow. And tonight, after the dinner party her uncle was hosting for his neighbor's family, Andreas was going to get his wish. She blushed and hung up the phone.

Chapter Five

Saffron Fact: Saffron adulterators in Nuremberg were fined, imprisoned, and executed—by immolation—to keep the crop pure.

Rudolf and his wife and their son Lukas arrived precisely on time. To the minute, to the second. It must be a German thing, Savannah decided. Uncle Malcolm greeted them warmly at the door. The two men immediately began arguing about the age-old dilemma of screw caps vs. natural cork.

"You simply cannot tell the difference in taste," argued Uncle Malcolm. "There are fifty-three closing systems."

"Glass corks, plastic corks—closing systems don't affect the wine in a bad way," Rudolf protested.

"Rudolf, Annalise, it is wonderful to see you both. Welcome to my home. And Lukas, son, I can't wait until you meet my niece."

Savannah frowned and adjusted her bow. Her uncle was already calling Lukas "son." That was dangerous and a bit premature. She hadn't even met the man.

When she first laid eyes on Lukas, he seemed less than enthusiastic about being present. No doubt his parents had dragged him to the rendezvous. Savannah appraised him from behind a wide living room chair. From the looks of Lukas, he wouldn't have trouble getting his own dates. There were probably long lines of fräuleins waiting in the wings for his attention. From her vantage point, she couldn't determine what was wrong with him. He was the perfect specimen of a man. Too perfect. Too much like Sullivan Granger. His looks advertised, "I'm available, to any woman who wants me. *Every* woman."

"Ah, there you are, Savannah," Uncle Malcolm called. "Why are you hiding in the dark? Come out and meet our guests."

Savannah straightened her shoulders and walked toward the guests like she was walking to the guillotine. *Might as well get this over with.*

She locked eyes with Lukas and suddenly he broke into a smile. He came over and took her hand. "Savannah, what a surprise. You...you're, I mean—"

"You mean I'm not the charity case you thought I'd be."

Lukas was tongue-tied. "I didn't... I never... You aren't what I expected, no."

Savannah laughed.

"Children, come out on the balcony," Aunt Ilsa called. "We've got some appetizers and wine out here."

"Lukas, you have to see the view from here," his father said.

"We're coming, Father," Lukas said, grabbing Savannah's hand.

"When my father proposed this meeting, I did everything I could to get out of it. I thought you'd be—I mean, I was sure you would be—"

"A fat, ugly cow?"

"Well, maybe," Lukas admitted.

"You can let go of my hand now."

"No. I don't think I can," said Lukas, and he didn't.

"Lukas, look out here." Uncle Malcolm's hand swept in a wide arc. "Here you get a view of our two properties. Kleppinger and Baeder Vineyards. As far as the eye can see. I've always had a dream to unite the two properties."

Lukas whispered to Savannah. "I'd like to unite our two properties, too, as soon as possible."

Savannah blushed.

"And to think I almost didn't come."

"We make fine vinegars on the estate, as well as wine," Malcolm explained to Savannah. "And we grow white asparagus. It's always in demand when it's in season. Right now we have special plastic sheeting covering the crops, to limit the amount of light so they don't turn green. In the next three or four weeks, they will be ready for people to start eating them. They're a real delicacy. We bottle them, pickle them, and preserve them, and send them all over the world. We also grow corn as animal feed. Canola is huge for its oil. People also grow canola to be used as bio fuel. Austria is moving away from conventional sources of energy. We want to get rid of nuclear energy and replace it with renewable sources like wind energy and solar power. As a Sustainability major, I thought you'd appreciate that. You can put your degree to work."

"Yes, that's very commendable, Uncle Malcolm."

"We grow very special grapes, and we're increasing our organic wines," Malcolm noted. "We don't use any chemicals in our processes. We are not officially licensed to be organic, but we are, just the same. Our grapes are good for eating. The symbol outside our wine tavern—our Weinstube—is the symbol of a grape. It goes back to the time when people couldn't read and write, so we had pictures of pigs on the butcher shop door and grapes on the entrance to a winery. And did you know we use our more developed grapes to make wine vinegar? We add spices, herbs, and honey brought in from many parts of the world, and we even grow a little saffron here, like we produced in the Middle Ages, to flavor our vinegars.

"Did you know your Aunt Ilsa cooks the most amazing dishes with vinegar?" Malcolm continued. "You wouldn't believe it. She's a gourmet cook. She makes a sweet potato soup that tastes like heaven. And a tomato risotto with shrimp and fried capers fit for a king. Her vinegar chicken with oven potatoes is remarkable. And for dessert, her drunken pears with vanilla vinegar sabayon and her chocolate cake would make the angels sing. And you must get her to teach you how to make the Esterhazy Tarte."

"Malcolm," Ilsa demurred.

"In fact, she's put on a few pounds, she's such a good cook, but then there's more of her to love."

Uncle Malcolm patted his wife on the backside and squeezed her stomach. She wriggled away, embarrassed.

"Uncle Malcolm, Aunt Ilsa is beautiful," Savannah said.

"Ilsa knows I'm just teasing."

"Why do you want to grow vinegar? It's so sour," Savannah said, attempting to change the subject.

"Not the vinegar we make here on the estate. It's fine vinegar, sweet enough to drink like a liqueur. We make more than forty kinds. We use only the best wines from our vineyards to make our vinegars. We are dedicated to time-honored traditions. You can use them with entrées, for cooking, and for fresh salads, in rich sauces, vegetables, sweets, and for sipping, as an aperitif, or digestive, between courses and in small doses. We also sell mustard."

"There's a lot to learn."

"Young Lukas here will teach you everything you need to know," Malcolm assured.

"Kleppinger's is one of the oldest wineries in Austria, and they produce some of the world's best Rieslings," Lukas pointed out.

"I think Andreas would be interested in talking to you about this. He's interested in growing organic products."

"All he cares about is saffron."

"That's not true. You and Andreas have a lot in common."

Malcolm shook his head.

"Who is this Andreas?" Lukas asked. "Should I be jealous?"

"No one," Malcolm answered. "A poor saffron farmer my niece met at a train station. He's latched on to her to get to me."

"Uncle Malcolm, that's not true."

Malcolm grumbled.

Lukas refused to drop Savannah's hand and kept toying with her bow. He pulled her away from the adults.

"You look like a schoolgirl in that bow, you know."

"That's what I've been told."

"It's very exciting—is that how you Americans say it? Very sexy. Dangerously sexy."

Savannah bit her lip.

"Like I can look but I can't touch. Like you're off limits, but it makes me want to touch you even more. Forbidden fruit."

"Perhaps we'd better have a drink," Savannah suggested in an attempt to get his mind off her bow and his hands off her body.

"Yes, I think I need to cool off a bit," Lukas agreed.

"Here, my boy. Try this." Uncle Malcolm placed a glass in Lukas's hand. "But you'll have to let my niece go for a moment."

Lukas released Savannah's hand and took the glass Malcolm offered. "Very smooth." He handed the glass to Savannah. "You must try this. It's excellent."

Savannah took a sip. "Delicious."

"Your father and I have been talking, and we think a merger of our families and all that entails makes perfect sense." Malcolm still stood next to them.

Lukas didn't take his eyes off Savannah. He encouraged her to take more of her drink.

"Uncle Malcolm," Savannah said, taking another sip of wine, "you sound like you're offering me to the highest bidder."

"I'm doing no such thing. I'm just opening your eyes to the possibilities. You can't deny, Rudolf, they would make beautiful children together. Savannah's quite a looker, like her mother."

Aunt Ilsa tightened her jaw.

"Uncle Malcolm! I think you're being rather obvious and premature."

"I have to agree with your uncle, Savannah," said Lukas. "I don't believe I've ever seen a more beautiful girl in my life. I am what you Americans call smitten."

"Thank you, but you hardly know me."

"And tonight we will rectify that. Come, sit with me. Tell me everything about yourself." He picked another glass of wine from the serving table and handed it to Savannah.

"I'm afraid I'm not all that interesting."

Lukas's eyes wandered to her breasts. "On the contrary, I'm captivated, Fräulein."

Savannah's nipples hardened involuntarily, and she moistened her lips. There was no doubt about it. Lukas Baeder was exactly the kind of man her mother would approve of. He had movie-star looks and charm to spare. His fortune assured him of a successful future. It would also make Uncle Malcolm happy.

"Go on, drink some more wine," Lukas urged. "It's very sweet."

Savannah took a sip.

Lukas leaned in and gently kissed her lips. "Yes, very sweet."

"Are you trying to get me drunk?"

"Is it working?"

"I'm afraid I'm not much of a wine drinker."

"We'll have to do something about that."

"I think you're trying to take advantage of me."

"I'm not what you Americans call a wolf. I'm attracted to you, Savannah. Do you feel the same way?"

"Lukas, we just met."

"We have all night to get acquainted, and tomorrow we have a full working day. Your uncle has asked me to show you around his properties and explain the wine-making and vinegar-making processes. There's a private vinegar cellar and herb chamber where the vinegars ferment and mature. They are lit by candlelight. Very romantic, I think. There's a lot to learn, and I'm a very good teacher. Very patient. We will do a vinegar tasting. The unique Kleppinger brand of fig vinegar is sinfully delightful when drunk pure. And of course, there's the Romeo brand, your uncle's own, a romantic seducer that hardly knows any limits. It exudes a wealth of flavors of wild oranges, lavender, cinnamon, cardamom, elderberry blossoms, and other enticing herbs. It is a stimulating aperitif. And then there's our—I mean, your—Madonna vinegar with a kiss of wild cherries, sour cherries, apricots, and vanilla to give it a sensual touch. It is simply heavenly."

Savannah rolled her eyes at the not-so-subtle innuendos and felt as if Lukas were about to do some touching and tasting of his own. "Are we still talking about the vinegar?"

"Did you know that in the Old Testament, the fig was a sacred and noble fruit?"

"No, I did not. You're just a font of information. And that's very generous of you. But actually, I have an engagement right after dinner. I'm meeting someone."

"Andreas?"

"A friend," Savannah said.

"Cancel it."

"That's rude."

"Then promise me you'll save the day for me tomorrow. I'm afraid your uncle will insist. And afterwards, I'll show you around town. A private tour."

"I don't know." Lukas was beginning to get uncomfortably possessive. "How is it that you know so much about my uncle's business?"

"He and my father are best friends, and I think he

47

hopes that one day I would, that is, *you* would inherit his estate and combine it with my family's neighboring estate by our union, that we would unite our two families as well."

"I see."

Lukas pulled out his cell phone and tapped it. "Savannah. Your name means flat, tropical grassland. You are anything but flat." He focused on her nipples, and his eyes began to glaze over.

"Lukas, I think you've had too much to drink."

"I admit, I was drunk before I came. I thought if I drank enough wine our meeting would be more palatable."

"And now?"

"I am overcome by your beauty and grace," said Lukas, placing his wine glass on the table before he slid slowly out of his chair and onto the blue flagstone patio.

"Uncle Malcolm, I think we have a problem."

Chapter Six

Saffron Fact: Saffron was used by ancient Persian worshippers as a ritual offering to their gods and as a perfume and a medicine.

The next time he saw her, Savannah had changed into tight-fitting jeans and an alluring sheer silk white shirt. There was a cool breeze floating in the air, and Savannah's nipples were standing erect. Andreas couldn't take his eyes off them.

"Sorry, I'm late," Savannah apologized.

"I would wait forever for you," Andreas promised.

Savannah had heard enough flattery for one night. Between Lukas and Andreas, she didn't know if their words were sincere or hyperbole. She'd had too much to drink and she wasn't thinking straight. After Lukas had passed out and his parents extended their apologies to her aunt and uncle and to her, she snuck out of the house to meet Andreas.

But not before her uncle had exacted a promise to give Lukas another chance.

"What did you think of him?"

"He was very impressive, before he passed out."

"But do you think there could be something between you? He certainly seemed interested."

In my breasts, she thought, remembering how he was ogling her. Like he couldn't wait to get his hands and his mouth on her. She felt lightheaded.

"I will agree to see him again," Savannah had said. "That's all I can promise you. He has offered to 'train' me all day tomorrow and familiarize me with your properties and operations."

"Wonderful." That had seemed to satisfy her uncle.

She turned her attention back to Andreas.

"What shall we do?" he asked.

"I'm rather tired. Perhaps we should call it a night."

"But you just got here. How was the dinner? How was Lukas?"

"He was overcome by my beauty," she said, laughing, remembering his flattering words before he passed out.

"Naturally. Do I have anything to worry about?"

"Not if you can hold your liquor."

"Because I am willing to fight for you," Andreas said, impassioned.

"I don't think that will be necessary."

She took a good look at Andreas. As a physical specimen, compared to Lukas, he was nothing to write home about. He wasn't particularly tall. His shoulders were not as broad. He wore glasses. He was definitely the studious type. His brown hair was unruly, and he continually swept away a loose strand that dangled down his forehead. Not exactly an alpha male, but then she was more partial to betas anyway.

But there was something familiar about him. Something safe. She felt comfortable around him. He was genuine. In comparison, Lukas seemed insincere.

"Is that a new bow?" Andreas asked, fingering her hair clip.

"What is it with men and bows?"

"It's quite a turn-on. I mean, you look like an angelic schoolgirl in that bow, but your body betrays you. When I look at you I'm tempted to do devilish things."

Savannah blew out a breath. She was tempted to remove the bloody bow. Temptress was not the look she was going for. That was her mother's department. But every male she met was fixated on her bows and her breasts. Not that she didn't feel something for Andreas. She looked up at him and hoped he would kiss her. She was a little drunk, yes, and she felt a little naughty. Felt an almost primal urge to mate with Andreas. Somehow, she trusted him.

She looked through the car window and up at the stars. Her head lolled over and fell against Andreas's shoulder.

"Sweetheart," he said, nudging her gently. "You've fallen asleep again, and I wasn't even talking about saffron."

"Take me home, Andreas."

"But you just got here."

"Take me home with you," Savannah whispered.

"Oh, God in Heaven." Andreas looked petrified and overcome with happiness at the same time. Like he had just won the lottery.

"Do you mean it?"

"I really do." Then she started snoring softly, and he smiled. He mentally put his plans on hold. He had to make one final trip to the Melk Abbey library, and he needed to concentrate on his mission. He couldn't afford to be distracted. And Savannah Sutherland was a major distraction.

Chapter Seven

Saffron Fact: Saffron is reputed to contain a natural cancer-fighting element.

"So, Savannah, our first lesson will start." Lukas had her alone in the tasting room, like a cornered sparrow.

Savannah was having trouble concentrating. Lukas was easy to look at, but her thoughts kept wandering dangerously back to Andreas.

"Now, we will taste our Riesling." Lukas handled the first pour. "Ninety percent of all wines produced in this region are Rieslings." He handed her a glass.

She tasted the wine.

"What do you think?"

"Very dry."

"You have a good palate. That's correct." He offered her a basket of bread to cleanse her palate. Then he poured a second glass. "Now taste this one."

"This one is fruity-sweet," Savannah commented.

"Perfect."

She chewed another piece of bread. Lukas poured a third glass and set it on a table. She swirled the glass and sipped it. "Mmm. This is my favorite. Very fruity, very sweet."

Lukas sampled her lips when she had placed the glass on the table. Then his hands began to wander.

"Yes, it is. Just like you. You prefer the sweet. So do I."

Savannah pushed him away. "Lukas, keep your mind on the lesson and your hands to yourself, please."

Lukas smiled. "You are shy. I like that. But very soon you will not be pushing me away. We are destined to be together."

Savannah frowned. "How can you be so sure?"

"It is what your uncle desires, and I, as well. One day, we will manage our family estates together."

"What about what I desire?" Savannah tilted her head and tried to imagine working side by side, day by day, with Lukas on this vast estate. She couldn't. But she certainly could imagine working with sweet, unassuming Andreas. She got more satisfaction hearing him talk about his small saffron flower bed than she would ever get working on this vast estate with Lukas. And talk about beds—for some reason, she was physically attracted to Andreas. In fact, last night, she recalled thinking she wanted to remove his glasses, kiss his lips, and share his bed. But that was probably the wine talking. Lukas was an overbearing wolf. And she wouldn't go to him like a sheep to the slaughter, no matter what her uncle wanted.

"You will come around."

"You're very sure of yourself."

"I don't deny that. Now, for the second part of your training we will go up into the vineyards to look at the grape arbors. You might want to change shoes and put on a jacket. The vineyards are located on very steep slopes, and they run in vertical lines so we can take advantage of the smooth soil and the drainage. We're at the perfect elevation. The more north you get, the smaller the sun's inclination angle. But the vineyards are all walled off and protected. Each vineyard is carefully tended by the owners. Each produces its own brand of grapes. Kleppinger's is of course the oldest and the best. A very fine tradition. The Romans came and brought the wine to us. We prepare the vines in the summer and harvest in the fall. We also produce ice wine, which is very sweet."

"Ice wine? What is that?"

"The story is that a lazy monk indulged too much in drinking his own wine, and he waited too long to harvest his grapes, so they became rotten. It turns out when the grapes are frozen, the frost produces that rare, expensive ice wine, the highest quality, very rich and sweet, deep and complex. It goes well with hot and spicy foods or desserts. Now, many vintners wait until winter comes to harvest their grapes. Each grape has to be picked and processed while frozen. The grapes are harvested before sunrise. For quality ice wine, we need the perfect fruit, sunshine, and cold temperatures.

"It can get pretty cold out there picking the grapes for ice wine. It's not an easy life. We do our best. Sometimes we succeed, but we're never prepared for what life holds. It rains when it shouldn't rain. We may come back to harvest a month too late and the vines will be in bad shape. We are a family winery. We have today vineyards that Ilsa's grandfather planted. This business has been in Ilsa's family for seven generations. The Kleppinger name has been in this area for five hundred years."

"You sound as if you already own the Kleppinger estate."

"I apologize if I seem too forward, but I am excited by the possibilities. I am excited by the thought of our future."

Savannah rolled her eyes.

"Hundreds of years ago, most of the vineyards were owned by the church, the monastery, and no one else was allowed to harvest the grapes. They needed the wine for the service. You would need permission from the archbishop to grow your own wine," Lukas observed.

"All the grapes are handpicked," he explained. "The workers climb up and down the slopes. We don't use tractors. We currently cultivate fifteen hectares of vineyards on the banks of the Danube. One hectare is ten thousand square meters. A hectare can produce six to seven thousand bottles. Our particular location in the growing areas guarantees an especially long ripening season, promoting a distinctive grape aroma. The proximity to the Danube, the steep south-oriented slopes, and the slate in which the vines are rooted characterize the interplay of fruit and minerality in our wines. Our vines thrive on the slate."

"How did you learn so much about wines?"

"I went to university and apprenticed at two other wineries. But I learned more in the field from my father and from your uncle."

"Impressive, but I don't know if I can learn all this."

"You will. I will teach you. You'll see. Our relationship will ripen as the grapes on the vine."

Savannah was growing increasingly uncomfortable with his similes and his smooth moves.

"I am making you nervous," he stated.

"A little…uncomfortable," Savannah admitted.

"I apologize. But I don't hesitate to go after what I

want. When your uncle married into the Kleppinger wine estate, your Aunt Ilsa's father bequeathed his vineyards to them, and now they will come to you—to us, I hope. Although your uncle married into the business, he brought his own ideas and thoughts about the wine, and he improved it. And so will I. But we will remain dedicated to what our ancestors did before."

Lukas took Savannah into his arms and placed his lips on hers.

Lukas was an expert kisser, very practiced and polished. He didn't hesitate to use his tongue to try to arouse her. But his passion seemed contrived. She didn't want to be kissed by Lukas. She would rather save herself for Andreas. She pulled away.

"Let's get back to the subject at hand."

"Okay, I'm coming on too strong," Lukas apologized. "I can be patient."

Savannah seriously doubted that.

****

Andreas folded his hands and snarled. He felt like a jealous schoolboy. He had followed Savannah and Lukas up to the vineyards. They'd been cocooned in the Kleppinger offices for a long time, doing who knows what. He trusted Savannah, but Lukas was a slick character. He reminded Andreas of a snake, tempting Eve in the Garden. He was after one thing, possessing the Kleppinger properties, and with them, Savannah. She was very naïve and probably had no idea what was happening. Hopefully, Lukas wasn't plying her with wine until her head was spinning. They looked pretty close up there on the hillside. Too close.

When they started to descend, Andreas ducked out of sight. He couldn't afford to be seen and have

Savannah think he was spying on her—which, of course, he was. Or that he was possessive, which, apparently, he was.

That Lukas was a handsome fellow, no doubt. And he had a lot to offer. Any girl would probably swoon at his feet. But Savannah wasn't just any girl. She was everything to him. He already thought of her as his, and Lukas was presenting a formidable obstacle. An obstacle he would have to overcome.

Andreas, on the other hand, wasn't particularly swoon worthy. He was smart and single-minded. Usually, he would have been content to wait. He had always believed that good things come to those who wait. But since he'd met Savannah, he couldn't afford to wait. He had some urgent business to take care of. Then he was going to make her his.

Chapter Eight

Saffron Fact: Buddhist monks in India began wearing saffron-colored robes more than 2,000 years ago. Saffron is still widely used around the world as a fabric dye. Persian saffron thread has been found interwoven into ancient royal carpets and funeral shrouds.

Shielding his eyes from the glare of the sun with his right hand, Andreas looked up at the magnificent structure before him. It resembled a palace. In fact, this most famous abbey in Austria, founded in 1089, had originally been a castle. It was presented to the Benedictine monks by Leopold II in 1089, and a monastic school was founded there in the twelfth century. But he knew from the guidebooks it wasn't built in its current Baroque architectural style until between 1702 and 1736 by Jakob Prandtauer.

With the sunlight flooding in through the transom windows, Andreas felt he was truly in the presence of God, although, as a scientist, God hadn't figured into his life much at this point. But he found the abbey church awe-inspiring with its frescos by Johann Michael Rottmayr and the library with its frescos by Paul Troger.

Of course the abbey was impressive, but there was only one reason Andreas was attracted to it and one reason he kept returning. In 1797, the local abbey had published a manual on the cultivation of saffron crocuses.

His primary focus was the main library, famous throughout the world for its mega-manuscript collection, with its 16,000 ancient books (many of them at least 500 years old), and for its scriptorium, a major site for the production of manuscripts.

The private monastic library, designed by Charles McKim, was built in 1906, and consisted of twelve rooms containing about 1,888 manuscripts, 750 printed works before 1500, 1,700 works from the sixteenth century, 4,500 from the seventeenth century, and 18,000 from the eighteenth century. Together with the newer books, there were approximately 100,000 volumes in all.

Knowledge was precious to the monks. He was intimately familiar with the main library and the small library behind it. And that's where he was headed.

The monks had made an exception for Andreas to their policy of visits only with a guided tour, to allow him to pursue his research. Normally, the place was locked down as tight as a vault, literally under lock and key. Visitors had to be escorted through each room of the museum, out onto the overlook, and into the library, the second most sacred place in the monastery, besides the church. In fact, the first time he had set eyes on the library, he'd sworn, "*Ach, mein Gott!* This library must have cost a king's ransom." Little did he know how accurate he was.

Andreas parked his rental car on the grounds of the thousand-year-old abbey, a property almost as old as Austria itself. It was a hike to get to the imposing structure, but he was in good shape and he had done it dozens of times over the past year. If pressed, he was certain he could walk the path blindfolded.

He couldn't wait to get back to the book. The book held the key to the mystery. And the mystery had nothing to do with saffron. He had puzzled over one line in the manuscript, playing it over and over in his mind, until one day he realized what was bothering him. He was a bit of a history buff, and that one line had been niggling at his subconscious:

....the Abbot took possession of the ransom for the King of England in early 1193.

The facts about King Richard's return from the Third Crusade and subsequent capture were often contradictory, but most historians agreed Richard the Lionheart was apprehended by his enemy Duke Leopold of Austria's men a few days before Christmas in 1192 and locked in Dürnstein Castle, a stronghold on the Danube. After almost a year of negotiations for his release, Queen Eleanor of Aquitaine, the King's mother, paid the astronomical sum of 100,000 marks for her son's release. Scholars were also clear about the date of the King's ransom and eventual release from Ochsenfurt in early February 1194, almost a year later. It was there that English emissaries, abbots of Boxley and Robertsridge, located the king and began the lengthy diplomatic negotiations for his ransom and release. That process took the better part of a year.

According to the monk's manual, the emperor demanded 150,000 marks (100,000 pounds of silver) be delivered to him before he would release the king. A historical discrepancy? It made sense that it would take a great deal of time to negotiate a ransom and release.

Richard was passed from stronghold to stronghold. Once his capture was known to England, his whereabouts were uncertain. It would have taken time to catch up with the king.

But if the monk who had written the manual was to be believed, Eleanor of Aquitaine had started immediately to raise the ransom for her favorite son. Both clergy and laymen were taxed for a quarter of the value of their property, the gold and silver treasures of the churches were confiscated, and money was raised from taxes. Although the conditions of the king's captivity were not severe, according to the history books, his mother would not have let her favorite son languish in prison for a year.

So what happened to the first ransom? Was it stolen? And if so, by whom? Why wasn't Richard released earlier? He planned to have a talk with the abbot.

Only a seventy-five-minute drive west from Vienna, the Melk Abbey library had been Andreas's "home" for the past year. He'd arrived by bus, by boat, by train. He'd approached the abbey from many perspectives: in a private minivan tour on a boutique cultural day trip from his home in Vienna to the Wachau Valley, combined with wine tastings, biking, and sightseeing strolls in Dürnstein, walking the apricot trail, and viewing the abbey from the outside from a cruise on the Danube from Spitz to Melk. He was familiar with most of the area's medieval villages, ruins, and castles in the most romantic area of the country, and the Melk Abbey was located along one of Europe's ancient trading routes.

Mostly he arrived by train from Wien's

Westbahnhof or the REX train direct to the Melk train station, which ran a couple of times per day and took only one hour and fifteen minutes. From the train, he took a footpath to the abbey. He practically knew the steps by heart. If it was a beautiful spring day, he opted for a boat ride downstream from Melk to Krems, where he hopped aboard a train from Krems back to Wien's Franz-Josefs-Bahnhof. Today, his trip was short since he was coming from nearby Dürnstein.

Every visit to the abbey left him awestruck by the splendor he encountered. How could one describe such a treasure? He was astonished by the marble columns, the onion-domed towers, and the Baroque architecture of the ancient Benedictine monastery, and mesmerized by the gold-plated pulpits and wood carvings and the breathtaking view across the Danube. And, of course, the jewel in the crown—the monks' library, packed with shelves and shelves and galleries of precious leather-bound volumes and the infamous ceiling fresco. It must have cost a fortune to build and stock. Where did all that money come from?

The first time he'd visited the library, he began with a guided tour through the monastery's museum with its gold statues, the church with its gold-plated pulpits, the marble hall with its Paul Troger ceiling painting and delicate spiral staircase that put Vienna's Schönbrunn Palace's grand ballroom to shame. The Benedictines' lifestyle was ascetic. Their church was not. Wandering through gallery after gallery, confronted with such splendor in the medieval church, his first thought had been, "Who paid for such riches?"

With subsequent visits to the library, he'd gotten to know the two dozen Benedictine monks at Melk, and in the summer he had the option and the freedom of visiting the abbey on his own, bookshelf after bookshelf just waiting to be explored.

Before entering the library, he'd wandered again through the monastery museum, which traced the life of St. Benedict, the founder of Melk Abbey, and told visitors about the way of life of Benedictine monks who had lived and worked there. Sacred objects and stunning gold statues stood in modern mirrored rooms. Room after room was sealed off as tight as the Tower of London. The tour guides ushered stragglers into the next room and locked the doors behind them with oversized keys. What were they hiding?

It was in a local pub in Vienna that he'd first heard talk that Crusaders brought saffron to Lower Austria and stories of a monk's manual at nearby Melk Abbey about the cultivation of saffron, a spice that was no longer produced in the region. A vicar owned the pub, and you couldn't get to the church without going through the pub. The church itself had no doors of its own.

When he'd taken the train to Melk Abbey and inquired in the ancient library about the book, the monks had no idea what he was talking about. But he wouldn't give up. It had taken awhile, but he'd finally found not one but two obscure books, complete with color charts and technical information, that depicted saffron production in the region. It seemed like destiny to Andreas, so he decided to bring saffron cultivation back to life.

When Andreas discovered the manuscripts, he hit the research jackpot. But the books were too delicate to make photocopies. Books weren't allowed to be taken out of the library, and no cameras were allowed, so, respectful of the rules, he began the lengthy and tedious process of copying the manuals by hand, the way the monks used to.

No matter how much he traveled, the Abbey never ceased to surprise and delight him. It was his home away from home. That is, until he prepared for his permanent move to Dürnstein. He loved Vienna, it had so much to offer, but something was missing—his connection to the land. He began to tire of the familiar—the countless meetings, speeches, conferences. He hungered to feel his fingers in the dirt, to reconnect with something. He'd gone to Dürnstein for a day trip, to unwind, and found a kind of peace he hadn't felt in a long time. That was the spot, the one spot in all the world—and he had traveled around the globe—that he wanted to call home.

Dürnstein was close enough to his family in Vienna, and to a certain attractive Scottish lass he hoped might become part of the picture.

He recalled his last evening with Savannah. She had fallen asleep on him, snoring her little heart out. She sighed as though they had made contact. He risked kissing her lips and she smiled in her slumber, but she was in no state to make love. He would have to get her home.

He stopped by a bar and brought out a Styrofoam cup of coffee. He coaxed her to drink it. "I can't bring you home like this, Savannah. Your uncle would roast me on a spit or drown me in a wine vat or throw me deep in the Danube."

"Andreas, I want you to make love to me. I had it all planned, before I fell asleep. But if you don't want me…"

"Of course I want you, more than anything." She was opening herself to him and he was rejecting her, or that's what she was probably thinking. But he couldn't take advantage of her. He wanted nothing more than to undress her and make love to her. He wanted to rip her clothes off, to feel her nakedness against his body, to kiss her, to penetrate her. He wanted everything from her. He wanted to give her everything. But not like this. Not when she was practically in a semi-conscious state.

His hand hovered above her blouse. He wanted to taste her sweetness. But he held back. He was never going to get rid of this hard-on. Christ. She was tantalizing.

"Andreas," she sighed, reaching for him.

"Drink this coffee. And sober up. Then I'm taking you home."

"But—"

"Savannah, you are tempting me severely, but I need to take you home, now before I change my mind and do something we'll both regret. Come on, take a sip."

Savannah took the coffee cup with shaking hands and drank.

"Kiss me, Andreas." She looked up at him with pleading eyes. He could hardly resist her. But she didn't know what she was doing. And she didn't know what she was doing to him.

Andreas sighed and took her in his arms, placing the coffee cup in the cupholder between them. He kissed her, softly then hungrily. She was so responsive. She thrust her tongue into his mouth.

"You're a little devil," he whispered. "We must

stop, right this instant. I'm taking you home."

Savannah squirmed in his arms. "But I don't want to go home."

"Here, take another drink."

While she was drinking, he started the engine, drove to her uncle's house, and rang the bell. Christ, I hope Malcolm doesn't answer. How will I explain this? He'll take one look at me and he'll know. He'll think I'm a predator.

Fortunately, when the door opened, the housekeeper appeared.

"Put her to bed," Andreas ordered. "And don't tell anyone I was here."

Chapter Nine

Saffron Fact: Saffron is mentioned in ancient Chinese medical texts dating from around 1600 BC. In modern times saffron cultivation is promoted among Afghan farmers as an ideal alternative to opium production.

But Malcolm had seen the couple arriving from his bedroom window, Andreas supporting his niece, who appeared to be stumbling to the door, unable to walk under her own power. Malcolm tightened his hold on the wine glass, almost crushing it with his bare hands, as he peered down to the driveway at the sight below. Though the hour was late, he brought his cell phone and the wineglass into the bathroom, so Ilsa couldn't hear him and dialed his friend.

"Rudolf, are you awake?"

"Just enjoying a glass of Riesling."

"Listen, we need to do something about this Andreas Bauer character," Malcolm said, rubbing his chin thoughtfully. "I think my niece has developed feelings for him. If we don't take action now, this relationship could destroy our plans of uniting the two vineyards."

"My son is very taken with your niece. He's very serious about his intentions toward her. Savannah is a lovely girl. What do you propose?"

"Possibly we could engage some of our workers to pay him a visit, help him on his way out of town. He's already bought a place. We could burn it down. Or threaten to."

"How far are you willing to go?"

"Whatever it takes to get rid of him and keep him from pursuing my niece, a girl I think of as my own daughter. He's upsetting the delicate balance in our little corner of the Wachau. He's swept in like a wildfire, and if we're not careful he'll destroy our way of life like a weed destroying our vines. He's only one now, but if he captures a foothold, more will come. Today, he asks for a small tract of land. Tomorrow, who knows? We must preserve our vineyards at any cost."

The two men came to an understanding.

"Should we involve Lukas?" Rudolf wondered.

"Not for now. Let us preserve his plausible deniability."

"Of course."

"Let's drink to that," Malcolm said, raising his glass. Malcolm heard Rudolf clink his glass against the phone in agreement.

Chapter Ten

Saffron Fact: Saffron made its way to the New World when thousands of people fleeing religious persecution in Europe settled mainly in Pennsylvania and became known as the Pennsylvania Dutch. By 1730, these settlers were cultivating saffron after corms were first brought to America—in a trunk. They successfully marketed their product to Spanish colonists in the Caribbean. The price of Pennsylvania Dutch saffron was once listed on the Philadelphia commodities exchange, its value equal to that of gold.

Before he fell asleep, Andreas Googled Savannah's mother's bow shop and discovered it wasn't just some single brick-and-mortar operation in Charleston, but a digital powerhouse in the business world with assets to rival a successful Silicon Valley start-up. Why hadn't she told him? Well, to be fair, he was keeping some pretty big secrets himself.

After reading some of the articles online, he got the impression that Dina Sutherland was a highly respected entrepreneur. Savannah would be giving up a lot to dig up dirt with him in Dürnstein. She had multiple options. She could pursue a career and put her Sustainability degree to use or go into her mother's very successful "bow" business. Or take her uncle up on his offer to go into the winemaking business. If she chose that route, it would come with strings attached. Strings by the name of Lukas Baeder. And what about her father? Maybe he had other plans for her.

What could he, Andreas, offer Savannah? His saffron venture was just a dream at this point. He was also aware that Savannah preferred to live in Scotland. She had some choices to make. Was it fair of him to ask her to give up everything she loved for an uncertain future? How could he compete? Then there was the question of her feelings for him. He was in love with her. Did she return that love?

Chapter Eleven

Saffron Fact: Modern studies have shown the high levels of antioxidants found in saffron may help ward off inflammation in the body and that it may be helpful in treating sexual dysfunction.

Andreas and Savannah were at his house and he was regaling her with more tales of saffron. He hoped he wasn't boring her.

She was helping him line the shelves in his kitchen and in the shop. Savannah was proving to be a very good partner and a good listener. She seemed genuinely interested in saffron.

"Did you know there was a Saffron War?"

"They fought a war over saffron?"

"Yes. It lasted fourteen weeks and was started when an eight-hundred-pound shipment of saffron, valued at today's prices at more than $500,000, was hijacked and stolen by nobles on the way to Basel, Switzerland. The shipment was eventually returned, but trade in the thirteenth century was subject to mass piracy on a widespread basis. Thieves and pirates would often ignore gold and instead steal saffron marketed in Venice and Genoa, bound for Europe. So Basel began to plant its own saffron corms, which made it extremely prosperous among European towns."

"Tell me again how saffron made its way to

Austria?" Savannah asked, remembering what he had told her, but never tiring of hearing his voice.

"Saffron has been grown in Lower Austria from around 1200 well into the nineteenth century," said Andreas. "Saffron cultivation in Europe declined steeply following the fall of the Roman Empire. For several centuries after, saffron cultivation was rare or non-existent throughout Europe. This was reversed when Moorish civilization spread to the Iberian peninsula as well as to parts of France and Southern Italy. Saffron was rare, expensive, and in demand.

"But the saffron business is full of fraud," warned Andreas. "Be careful when buying saffron. Not even the highest price will guarantee the best quality. When you're buying saffron, you have to look out for the red flags. First, long red threads—this means that the thread has been dyed. Second, a very uniform red color—this also indicates the thread has been dyed. Third, streaks of yellow across the thread—this can happen when saffron is dyed, when one thread is covered by another, causing an uneven dying process.

"Saffron farming in Lower Austria was completely abandoned several decades ago, and I'm trying to identify appropriate farming techniques and re-establish the production of organically certified saffron in the region. I think it's important to develop an awareness of the history of saffron and reconnect with traditional saffron products. I've already started interviewing people to get written and oral testimonials from older people who have planted and harvested saffron."

"That sounds like a wonderful project." She had heard it all before, but she wouldn't dream of stopping him. He was so cute when he was talking about saffron.

"I have so many ideas."

"I know, and I love your passion for saffron."

"That's nothing compared with my passion for you." He came up behind her and pulled her close.

Savannah laughed. "You also love the idea of free labor in the kitchen and in your model garden."

He turned her around to face him. "When I get this venture off the ground, I'm going to hire some help. I don't expect you to work this hard for nothing."

"Andreas, I'm not complaining. I'm glad to be a part of your vision. I believe in what you are trying to accomplish."

He kissed her, and she responded but then pulled away.

"Now, don't distract me. We have a lot of work to do in here if we are going to get this kitchen up and running."

Chapter Twelve

Saffron Fact: Saffron was once prescribed as an antidote for the bubonic plague. When the Black Death struck Europe from thirteen forty-seven to thirteen fifty, demand skyrocketed. Plague victims desired it for medicinal purposes, but by then, most of the saffron farmers had died off.

Andreas whispered to the monk outside the abbot's office, although they weren't in the church so he wasn't sure why he was speaking so softly.

"I'd like to speak to the abbot, please."

"Is he expecting you?"

"Well, no, but it's important that I talk with him."

The monk's eyebrows drew together. He excused himself, and Andreas waited ten minutes before he reappeared.

"Come with me," he said.

The monk led him to another outer office and addressed a man at the desk. "Andreas Bauer to see the abbot."

"Herr Bauer. Have a seat. The abbot is on an important phone call. He'll be with you shortly."

Andreas had imagined what the daily life of a medieval monk might be like, specifically the monk who wrote the saffron manual. Back then, a monk's life adhered to a strict routine and discipline and was dedicated to worship, reading, and manual labor. The monks renounced all worldly life and goods, took the vow of poverty, the vow of chastity, and the vow of obedience. His monk would have attended church, spent his time reading from the Bible or the Book of Hours, the main prayer book containing prayers, psalms, hymns, and other readings, to be chanted at specific times of the day in private prayer and meditation. His work would have ceased at times of daily prayer. He would also have had chores like working hard on monastery lands, raising the necessary supplies of vegetables and grains, producing wine, ale, and honey and, Andreas had discovered, saffron.

Was he a cellarer? The monk who supervised the general provisioning of the monastery? His monk may have copied the manuscripts of classical authors, but in this case, he had penned his own manuscript.

Why would this monk, who he'd come to think of as *his* monk, know about the affairs of a king's ransom? Surely, the abbot, the head of Melk Abbey, would be privy to such information. When he'd read further, he discovered why. The ransom had been buried in the saffron field, where no one would be likely to look.

The librarian left Andreas sitting in a chair in the entryway. Within minutes, the secretary led him back to the abbot's office.

Andreas didn't know what to expect. A bare cell? These monks had taken the vow of poverty, but there was no evidence of poverty that Andreas could detect. The abbot's office was grand, almost to the point of being gaudy. Decorated in the Baroque style of the abbey, it held some paintings by well-known artists Andreas recognized, and from their signatures, they were originals. Was that a Gustav Klimt on the wall? Not very monk-like. Also a little risqué for what he imagined was a monk's taste, although he didn't doubt the possibility that the abbey had housed some unsavory characters through the ages. The church was not above reproach.

While Andreas was staring intensely at the Klimt, depicting a woman in gold wrapped in a sensuous embrace with a nobleman, the abbot approached him.

"Father Abbot," Andreas said, tearing his eyes away from the clinch and turning to shake the Reverend Father's hand.

"Herr Bauer, it's a pleasure to meet you," the abbot began. "I've wanted to meet the man who has spent the last year of his life at our library. We were thinking of putting in a cot or inviting you to join the order."

Andreas laughed.

"You're admiring our Klimt," continued the Reverend Father. "It was a gift. You look shocked. You're wondering why my office is so ornate. And what an abbot could find to like about a Klimt."

"Well, I—"

"Yours is a typical reaction. I assure you, I don't live this way. My living quarters are very austere. But people on the outside have expectations. And we have an image to uphold. Klimt is very Austrian. But then you know that, as you are from Vienna. As it turns out, I am very fond of Klimt. We tend to want what we can't have."

Was he referring to the painting itself or the passion depicted in the painting?

"That's none of my concern," Andreas assured, wondering how the abbot knew he was from Vienna.

But then he supposed everything that went on at the abbey was his business.

The Reverend Father offered his visitor a seat and he sat in his chair.

"So tell me, what is the purpose of this meeting?"

Andreas got right to the point. "I've located two books in the Small Library which deal with saffron production. One dates back to 1776 and the other to 1797. The brother I've been dealing with was not even aware these manuals existed."

The abbot leaned back in his seat, inhaled, and steepled his hands. "I know that at one time the saffron from Lower Austria was considered to be one of the best available in Europe. Merchants came from all over Europe to visit the seed market in Krems. Approximately eight hundred kilograms of saffron was being produced in the mid-eighteenth century. Our fields here at Melk were among the highest quality in the area. And since 1850, the industry has been all but forgotten."

"That is correct. You are very well informed."

"What is your interest in our saffron manuals, Herr Bauer?"

"I'm a botanist, and I've decided to revitalize saffron production in the Wachau. These books tell me how to do that, step by step."

The Reverend Father stroked his beard. "It's no secret I've been trying to locate those books ever since I got here. There were no books filed under "S."

"That's because they were filed under C for *Crocus Austriacus*."

The abbot pursed his lips. "Ah. They were well hidden. So what can I do for you?"

"Those weren't the only things that were well hidden. I had some questions. There were some discrepancies. I wonder if you could satisfy my curiosity."

"What were the nature of these *discrepancies*?"

"The monk who wrote the manual talked of a delivery of a king's ransom, Richard the Lionheart's ransom, to be exact, in 1193."

"1193, that's correct. And?"

I'm afraid you have your dates confused. The king's ransom was paid in 1194. But according to the manual, there were two ransoms paid. One paid by Queen Eleanor of Aquitaine while her son was imprisoned in Dürnstein. The second a year later in 1194."

"But the king was not released in Dürnstein."

"Exactly. There is no mention of a first ransom in any history book."

"And this was documented in a monk's manual on saffron?"

"Yes, it was quite detailed. He reported that the ransom was arranged through the abbot at Melk Abbey and delivered to the abbey, and that the Abbot instructed a monk to bury the gold and silver in one of the abbey's outlying saffron fields."

The abbot heaved a sigh. "Did he also report that the clergy was taxed for a quarter of the value of its property, and that the gold and silver treasures of the church were confiscated? Much of that money rightfully belonged to the Benedictine church."

"Meanwhile, the money to rescue the king, that was to be transferred to the Duke of Austria, was never received by his ambassadors. If it was 'lost' along the way, Richard would be held responsible. So he languished in prison for another year, until they transferred him to another fortress and the second ransom was paid."

The abbot drilled Andreas with his eyes. "And what do you suppose happened to that money, that *first* ransom, if it ever did exist?"

"I have some idea, but I wanted confirmation from you."

The abbot pursed his lips. "Tell me what you think you know."

"The monk, who was alive when new construction on the building was started, maintains that the treasure remained buried until 1702, when it was dug up to fund the magnificent structure Melk Abbey is today in its current Baroque architectural style by Jakob Prandtauer. The private monastic library, designed by Charles McKim, was built in 1906. Such monumental undertakings would require a great deal of money. Two to three times the annual income of the English Crown, to be exact."

"That's pure speculation." The abbot shifted in his seat. "How could the monks who authored manuals in 1776 or 1797 know what occurred in 1193?" His face remained inscrutable but his actions indicated he was agitated.

"Apparently, it was a well-guarded and well-documented secret among the monks and abbots through the centuries," Andreas continued. "Rumor has it that Richard was so expensive to feed and house, with all the food and wine he and his party consumed, that they finally returned him without the ransom. No one could afford to keep him for long, so they moved him from place to place, from stronghold to stronghold, until March 28th, when he was brought to Speyer and handed over to Henry VI, the Holy Roman Emperor, who imprisoned him in Trifels Castle. The money to rescue the king was transferred to the king's ambassadors on February 4th, 1194. Then he was released, after two years in captivity."

"Pure coincidence, speculation."

"I don't believe in coincidences."

"And what do you plan to do about your *discovery*?"

Andreas shrugged his shoulders. "Nothing."

"You realize that if this story were true—and I'm not saying it is—it could cause quite a conflict between Austria and the United Kingdom. It could be damaging to the church. I think it unwise to go spreading rumors that can't be proven."

"Is that a threat?"

The abbot sat up, stonefaced, and cracked his knuckles beneath his desk.

"Take it however you wish. I am a man of God."

"A lot of evil has been done in the name of God and the church," Andreas noted.

"Herr Bauer, I'm afraid you have been reading too many thriller novels."

"Perhaps. But I take my saffron growing seriously. I would hate to have any interference from the church."

"Then this conversation never happened. Is that understood?"

The abbot pressed his intercom without waiting for an answer. His secretary appeared at the door.

"Please accompany Herr Bauer back to the library and have him show you where the saffron manuals are filed. Then bring them to my office. Take them out of circulation. They are no longer available for public viewing."

Andreas counted his lucky stars that, toward the end, he had photographed both of the books, against all the rules, and had the copies safety secured. He had his insurance policy.

When the door to his office closed, the Reverend Father picked up his phone and dialed. The abbey had survived a number of threats throughout its history, but it would not survive this one. As the abbot prepared for daily Matins, his face twisted into a grimace. He was the current protector of the secret, and Andreas Bauer would have to be dealt with. Somehow, he had discovered proof of the first ransom. A fact known only by a few abbots and monks through the ages. A fact that, if made public, could destroy the abbey.

"Yes, Malcolm Sutherland, please. Tell him it's the Reverend Father from Melk Abbey. When he returns, tell him to call me immediately about an urgent matter concerning the Vinea Wachau vintners."

Chapter Thirteen

Saffron Fact: Today, the saffron plant is cultivated in countries from Spain, Italy, and Greece to India. Nearly 90 percent of the world's saffron is from Iran.

"Savannah," Andreas said. "It's good to hear your voice. I miss you."

"We just saw each other last night."

"It seems like longer. How was your day?"

"Lukas wore me out. We spent the day touring Uncle Malcolm's properties and meeting his staff, and he even had me working in the vineyard. I'm learning the business from the ground up, or from the grapes up, as he likes to say. I'm beat. I just want to soak my feet and pass out on the bed."

"I had hoped I could interest you in dinner."

"I'd love that, but my uncle has invited some friends over for dinner."

"Do those friends include Lukas Baeder, by any chance?"

Savannah hesitated. "How did you know about Lukas?"

"You talked about him while we were out last night."

"I don't remember mentioning him."

"I don't guess you do. I'd be careful. Your uncle is trying to play matchmaker. Why don't you blow off the dinner and come out with me?"

"Because I promised my uncle and I promised Lukas."

"Promised him what?"

"To give him another chance."

Andreas fumed silently.

"Andreas, are you jealous?"

"Is that a trick question?"

"No. It's just that Lukas had a little too much to drink the night we met, and he needs to make up for his bad behavior."

"Bad behavior?" Andreas raised his voice.

"We can see each other tomorrow. Andreas, are you still there?"

"Are you thinking of working with your uncle in the vineyard?"

"I haven't decided yet. I want to be open to the possibility, but not if Lukas is part of the deal."

Andreas blew out a breath. "That's encouraging. All right. But I need you the whole day. I'm going to put you to work."

"Doing what?"

"It's a surprise. And Savannah? Wear your work bow."

Savannah laughed. "I do have one. I have a bow for every occasion. Like a Girl Scout. I am prepared."

"I'll look forward to seeing you in it. I'll pick you up at nine in the morning."

Chapter Fourteen

Saffron Fact: Due to the manual harvesting technique, saffron is the world's most expensive spice per unit weight.

"So, Savannah. I promise to be on my best behavior tonight."

Lukas produced a beautiful bouquet of flowers from behind his back. "Beautiful flowers for a beautiful girl."

Savannah smelled them and took them from her guest. Lukas followed her into the kitchen while she arranged them in a crystal vase and placed them on the counter.

"They're lovely. Thank you."

Lukas placed a quick but possessive kiss on Savannah's lips.

"What do you say we ditch this crowd and go off somewhere where we can be alone."

"I thought you said you were going to be on your best behavior."

"I will be. I promise."

"Your parents will be disappointed."

"I assure you, they won't be, as long as we're together and getting along."

Lukas rubbed his hands slowly up and down Savannah's bare arms.

She twisted away from his grip.

"Don't be coy, Savannah. You know what's expected of us."

"I don't know what you mean."

"Your uncle, my father—they want us to be together."

"And what about what we want?"

"I'm willing to play."

"You think this is a game?"

"I admit, I was reluctant at first. But the moment I met you I fell hard. I want to move up the timetable. Let's give them what they want. Give me what I want."

Lukas pressed his body tightly against Savannah's, banded her with his arms, and captured her lips. She felt his erection grow hard against her.

She pushed him away.

"You think you're irresistible?"

"Most women do."

Savannah frowned. "I agreed to meet with you again because I promised to give you another chance. But your behavior continues to be inappropriate."

"Come on, Savannah. Don't be a tease. You come out wearing that low-cut silk number, baring your arms and practically everything else, with that body of yours and that bloody bow, and you expect me to put on the brakes?"

"I didn't dress this way for you."

"You're asking for it."

Savannah crossed her arms. "Lukas Baeder, you're a predator."

"And you're my prey," Lukas whispered, stroking Savannah's breast.

Savannah pulled away. "Okay, that's enough."

"Just a kiss to seal the deal," Lukas pleaded.

"There isn't going to be any deal."

"You don't know what you're giving up. The chance to merge two of the most successful wineries in the valley. We'll be a powerhouse. And you get me in the bargain."

Savannah laughed. "You have an overinflated opinion of yourself."

"I know my own worth," he replied, "and yours. You'll be sorry if you don't give me a chance."

"Not very likely."

"Your uncle has made up his mind."

"And I've made up mine. I'm going up to my room."

He grabbed her arm. "You sure you don't want some company?"

"Quite sure," she said, pulling away from him. "Please make my apologies to your family and the other guests."

As she made her way to the guest bedroom, she thought it was curious that she found Lukas's advances off-putting while she welcomed Andreas's touch. Those were the vagaries of attraction.

The minute Savannah walked into her room, her cell phone rang.

"Hello."

"Savannah, I'm just calling to make sure you're still free for tomorrow."

"Well, I'd planned to—"

"No, let me rephrase. I don't care what you're doing."

"Andreas, I—"

"Drop everything. I'll be over to pick you up first

thing in the morning. It's time. We're going to start planting."

****

Andreas clicked off the cell phone so Savannah wouldn't have a chance to argue. He had taken a trip to Wallis in Switzerland the day before, where the saffron was still grown according to centuries-old traditions. He'd bought 100 bulbs for his starter farm.

As soon as the sun rose he would text Savannah and confirm their rendezvous. Life was exciting, ripe with possibilities. He had perhaps acted brashly on the phone, but he was feeling confident and optimistic about life, particularly about life with Savannah. Lukas had her this evening. He had to let her know he was in contention.

Andreas arrived right on time the next morning. Savannah was waiting for him on the driveway. She wore blue jeans and a three-quarter-sleeved white cotton blouse. Her hair was pulled back and held in place with a denim bow the color of the sea and sprinkled with rhinestones.

When he saw her, his heart stuttered. He was dazzled. Damned if this bow didn't bring out the sparkle in her eyes.

"How many bows do you have?" he asked.

"One to match each outfit."

"Well, I like them. You look fetching. You have no idea what those bows make me want to do to you."

Savannah smiled and got into his car. "That was not my intention. I'm dressed to work. This is my working bow."

"I see. How was dinner last night?"

"I went to bed without eating."

"What about Lukas?"

"He went to bed hungry and angry." And *horny*, she relished.

"Good for him. You can tell me all about it later."

Andreas handed her a bag with a warm croissant and a Styrofoam cup. "I hope you like hot chocolate."

"I love hot chocolate. Thank you. Where are we going?"

"To my house. We're going to plant the model garden. I told you last night."

"You said it was a surprise. I was too angry at Lukas to listen."

Andreas kept his eyes on the road but stole occasional glances at his passenger. He was right where he wanted to be, with Savannah by his side. When they arrived at his house, he parked in the back.

"Everything is ready. I bought the bulbs in Switzerland, and I prepared the ground for planting. We won't need help because the model garden is so small. For the saffron to thrive, you must have a well-drained herbal bed exposed to a lot of sun, which we have right here."

"This is so exciting," Savannah remarked. "This is the beginning of your big dream."

You are my dream, Andreas thought, smiling at Savannah. She looked just right in his house, in his garden, her beauty bathed in the morning light. She looked like she belonged. Like they belonged together.

When he and Savannah arrived at his house, he laid out the plan.

"This is not a weekend pastime for me," Andreas asserted. "While now we only have a model garden, soon we will have a larger spread. This is the perfect place to start. The time is now. I will plant the flowers in the summer, and the saffron crocus will bloom in the fall in my garden."

"I don't know how much help I can be," Savannah protested. "I don't know how to plant saffron."

"Well, luckily I do, and I will teach you." Andreas handed her a pair of gardening gloves, a spade, and a straw hat. He brought her out to the model garden in front of his house and got down on his knees in the dirt with a box of saffron corms.

"You can grow saffron with seeds, but I prefer corms. Here's a picture of what the plant will look like when it blooms."

"What a beautiful purple bloom," Savannah said, admiring the photograph.

"First, the green leaves will emerge, followed by the flower. I will use a tweezer-like tool or just my fingernails to harvest them. The part of the plant we harvest are just these three reddish filaments. That's why it's so expensive."

"It hardly seems worth it."

"It is worth it. And the demand far outweighs the supply."

Andreas knelt on the ground and pulled Savannah down with him.

"You place the flat side of the bulb down and point the tip face-up, like this." Andreas demonstrated. "We'll dig the holes four inches deep and four inches apart so each bulb is covered with two to three inches of soil. Each bulb produces a few sets of leaves, and each flower only bears three stigmas, as I've said. It is very easy to plant, but not so easy to harvest. Here, now you try one."

"When did you say the flowers will come up?"

"Generally, six to eight weeks after we plant them. The blooms last about three weeks. We have to mark where we plant them because, in eight to twelve weeks, the leaves wither and vanish until they appear again in the fall," he said while Savannah dug a hole with her spade. "The bulbs must be planted in sandy-loamy soil with good drainage. If the soil is not well drained, the plants will rot. Saffron is a very labor-intensive crop. The costly spice is extracted from the flowers' pistils. If they're not harvested quickly, the flowers begin to wilt shortly after they open. And since the saffron crocus self-propagates in the soil, it grows from year to year. I've developed a new technique for when we're ready to harvest these. Then after the harvest I will refine and sell the products."

He continued, "The two of us can handle this garden, but once we get our field, we'll need helpers, like you need to grow and pick the grapes. This variety of crocus is special. It can't grow in the wild or reproduce without human intervention. These bulbs will produce bright orange-red stigmas of beautiful purple flowers. But they must be propagated and painstakingly harvested by hand and only on the morning they bloom. The more careful the cultivation, the higher the price. Then they must be kept in a cool, dry place."

"Why don't saffron farmers just sell saffron in its original form?"

"For the same reason the top winemakers like your uncle don't sell their grapes in the supermarket, only the wine, and then they can sell it for more. The commodities shouldn't be sold too cheaply. Developing those products and bringing them to market creates value. In Greece and Italy, saffron production is coming to an end. I hope to preserve their techniques by describing and documenting them. Otherwise, the last remaining saffron farmers in Europe will decline even more. As for our fields, the corms will reproduce if we dig them up every two years and divide them. We will do that in May or June. They should be fertilized at the beginning and end of the season."

When they were through planting, Savannah stood up and stretched.

"That was hard work."

"Would you like to use my shower to wash the dirt off?"

"Yes, I really need to."

Andreas got a fluffy towel from the hall closet and left a wrapped bar of soap and some shampoo in the shower.

"I'll be downstairs in the kitchen if you need me."

When Savannah came downstairs, Andreas took his turn in the shower. He wondered what it would be like to shower with her. He knew he couldn't wait much longer to be with her. But he needed a signal that she was ready, one when she was not drinking and was in a proper state of mind.

It had been a long, exhausting, but exhilarating day. He and Savannah sat on rocking chairs on the front porch, like an old married couple. They gazed at each other and smiled. He reached for her hand.

"What are you thinking?" Andreas wondered.

"That this is exactly where I want to be. It feels safe. When I was growing up, I was shuttled from one side of the ocean to the other, back and forth, from South Carolina to Scotland, year after year. I never had a permanent home. During the school year I made friends, but then every summer I was pulled away and those friends found new friends and I had to start over. I don't want my children to feel that way. That's why I'm not sure I want children. I never had a real family. I never saw my parents together. I felt I had to take sides, to choose between my mother and my father. In the end, my mother made the choice for me. She was busy building her empire. My da had more time for me. I loved my home on the lake in Scotland. It was a fairy tale life. Then I had to go back to my mother. I just wanted to belong to someone. And to be loved. To have stability and to put down roots. I don't want to be some delicate flower that drifts across the land with the wind."

"Then that is what I want for you. Why did you break off your engagement?"

"My fiancé wanted children and I didn't, not right away and maybe not ever."

But she could visualize Andreas's large, capable hands folded around her son or daughter's smaller hands, patting the earth, planting saffron flowers together. The boy would be studious and smart like Andreas, with a lock of brown hair falling over his eyes. The girl would wear a bow and be the apple of her father's eye. She had never thought of having children, until this moment, until she met Andreas.

"What are you thinking?" Savannah asked.

"I'm thinking that if I don't kiss you again, I might explode."

Savannah laughed. "That's very dramatic. Why don't you go ahead and kiss me, then."

Andreas stood up and lifted Savannah to her feet.

He took her in his arms and brushed his lips against hers, drawing her ever closer. "Do you want me to stop?"

"N-no," she mumbled.

He wanted to rush headlong into the vortex, but was it too soon?

Savannah made the next move. She wound her arms around Andreas's neck and nuzzled him. "Don't stop."

Andreas had been dreaming about making love to Savannah since he saw her standing at the train station. He could hardly hold back. He bent down and kissed her lips gently, then more urgently, and he went on kissing her. He rubbed her back in a circular motion. She responded by nestling her body against his.

"Savannah," he whispered.

"Andreas," she responded.

She had changed into one of his old T-shirts and had discarded her sweat-stained bra. He could feel her breasts straining against the fabric, and he cupped them in his hands until her nipples came erect.

She whimpered and thrust her breasts against his chest.

"Not here," he cautioned.

"Andreas," she begged.

"Sweet Savannah, I want you, too, you have no idea how much, but do you think it's wise to be seen out here?"

"Then take me inside," she demanded, placing fluttering kisses on his lips.

Andreas frowned, but his body was heating up like a furnace.

He lifted her off her feet, like a bride, his bride, and

opened the door of the little house, a house he now thought of as their house.

"Lucky for us, it comes furnished," Andreas stated, carrying her upstairs into the bedroom.

He deposited her on the bed. "Are you sure about this?"

Savannah answered by stripping off her clothes, carefully removing her blue jeans and his T-shirt. He began fondling her, sucking first on one nipple, then the other, while he slipped off her panties and attempted to remove his jeans. She gasped and then slowly finished helping him undress.

His hands cupped her center until she bucked wildly and called out his name, naked and thrashing.

"Andreas, I want—"

"Tell me what you want."

"I want to be closer to you, but I don't know what to do," she whispered.

"Then I'll show you."

Did she mean she'd never been with a man? She was young. That was possible, but she was very passionate for such an inexperienced girl.

"Touch me here," Andreas said, bringing her hand to his center, instructing her.

She obeyed, rubbing him slowly, torturing him. If he didn't enter her soon, he would explode. She was wet and ready. What a vixen. There was no way this was her first time.

He stuck a slender finger in her opening and then another until her eyes glazed over.

"Andreas, please."

She was very tight. Was it possible she was a virgin?

Then he looked at the bow in her hair and almost came right there.

"I have to have you, now," he cried, turning her onto her back and entering her. She was tight all right, too tight, but he kept up a steady rhythm. Her hands dug into his back and she arched her body up to meet him.

He had started out slowly, but he couldn't take much more. His tongue lashed her nipples, and then he mounted her and buried himself in her warmth. "Oh, God, Savannah."

They cried out at the same time.

Damn, he hadn't used a condom. It wasn't as if he kept a supply of them in a drawer or carried them around in his wallet. He wasn't a ladies' man. And he hadn't come here to deflower a maiden. He didn't have time for women. His mission was saffron, but right now, here in this bed, his heart beating like a caged lion, he could see only Savannah.

He stayed inside her, collapsing on her stomach.

A steady flow of tears trickled down her face and she licked them off.

"Savannah, sweetheart, what's wrong? I didn't hurt you, did I?"

"I've never done this before," she admitted.

He rolled over and off her and brought his hands to her face.

"This really was your first time? But you were engaged."

She nodded. "I was. And he wanted to make love, but something stopped me. I didn't want to make the same mistake my mother made, falling in love with the wrong man. And I didn't want to get pregnant. We were close, but we never… I mean, I never let him… But with you, it was different."

"I wouldn't have known. You were so willing. Did you enjoy it?"

She hid her face in his neck.

"You did, I could tell. I'm sorry I wasn't more gentle. But you drove me mad."

Savannah licked her lips. "I liked it when you…"

"Show me," he urged.

"When you…"

She brought his mouth against her nipples. He sucked noisily.

"And I like that too." Andreas paused, smiling.

"But I'd better get back. My uncle will take one look at me and he'll know."

Andreas kissed her face and licked her tears away. "Don't worry about anything. It will be all right. You can tell him I'm going to marry you."

"Marry me?"

"Yes, I knew from the very moment I laid eyes on you in the train station that you were meant for me."

Savannah bit her lip. "You didn't use, aren't you supposed to use…"

"If you get pregnant, so be it. I want a family with you. Right away. I'm madly in love with you, Savannah."

And that very minute she didn't mind the idea of having a family with Andreas.

"And I love you, Andreas. I've never felt this way before. When can we do this again?"

Chapter Fifteen

Saffron Fact: Traditional Chinese medicine used saffron to improve blood circulation and to treat bruising.

Andreas walked outside through the thick blond oak double doors onto the pebbled patio and surveyed his garden. The bulbs were not yet in bloom. But soon the glorious purple flowers and the red stigmas would push through the earth. It would be a sight to see. It was a beautiful day.

He turned to face his building, squinting into the sun. His eyes took in the slate roof and the dark wood paneled front wall and his new sign, made up in Vienna and just delivered: *Wachauer Safran Manufaktur* in gold lettering against black, with the hours of operation, *Freitag – Sonntag 12-17 Uhr / Mitte April – Ende Oktober*.

And the sign he was most proud of: *Seminarraum*. On a chalkboard sandwich sign was written *Safran krokus im TOPF*, his potted saffron samples for visitors to buy and take home. Here he would deliver his lectures, and to the left of the classroom, the kitchen, where he would make the *Safran* products, and the shop where he would sell them.

Everything was coming together. He had the rest of the summer to convince Savannah to stay in Dürnstein with him. She was in love with him, he knew. But something from her past was holding her back.

He noticed a sudden movement at his left, and then they were upon him, three imposing shadows, a pack of human wolves, barking like mad dogs, kicking him, punching him, beating him with tornadic force until he was bloody, semiconscious, and doubled over in pain. How could something so right go so wrong?

His last thought before blackness enveloped him was, "Don't dig up the garden."

When he regained consciousness, Savannah was there beside him. He attempted to turn toward her, but he was so stiff he could hardly move. His head ached. He felt like he had a hangover, but he didn't remember drinking. An obscure fact came to mind: The ancient Romans believed that saffron and wine prevented a hangover in the morning. Perhaps all he needed for a cure was some saffron.

"W-what happened?"

"You don't remember? You were beaten."

"Where am I?"

"You're in the hospital. You've been unconscious for two days. You have a concussion and some broken bones. And some nasty-looking bruises, all over your face. You look a lot better than when they first brought you in. Today, you only look like a raccoon. Do you know who did this to you?"

Andreas shook his head. "I don't remember anything. They came from out of nowhere. It was so unexpected."

"The police were here asking questions, but I had no answers. Who would want to harm you?"

Andreas had a fleeting thought. Savannah's uncle?

But the attack had happened so suddenly he had no way to positively identify his attackers.

"My house. Did they do anything to my house?"

Savannah glanced at the floor. "I'm sorry, Andreas. They spray-painted your beautiful sign, did some damage to the classroom. Nothing that can't be repaired."

Andreas winced.

"And the garden?"

"Undisturbed. The leaves weren't up yet, so I doubt they knew there was anything under the dirt. They trampled the garden, but I don't think they did any damage."

"Thank God. Otherwise, we would have lost an entire growing season. How did you know I was hurt?"

Savannah placed her hand gently in Andreas's palm, one of the only places not wrapped in bandages. "You were supposed to pick me up and you didn't show. I knew something was wrong. So I called a taxi and had the driver take me to your house. The door was open, I saw the graffiti on the signs, and I went next door. Your neighbor said she saw them take you away in an ambulance, and I tracked you down."

"You came over in a taxi?"

"I didn't want to bother my aunt and uncle. But it was the strangest thing. The man driving the taxi picked me up at the estate, and when I asked him to take me to your house and I gave him directions, he started shaking, literally, like he was panicked. He was breathing heavily and sweating profusely. It got worse the closer we got to the Danube. I asked him what was wrong, and he said. 'I'm from Ghana. Not many people know this, but Ghanaian people are afraid of rivers. Are there crocodiles in this river?' " I told him I didn't think so, but that I'd just arrived in town and I didn't know for certain.

" 'In my land,' he said, 'you can bring a whole chicken and feed it to the crocodile and then he will let you pet him. I have a picture of this on my cell phone.' Then he started flipping through his phone while he was driving, and I said, 'Please, keep your eyes on the road.' But when we arrived at the hospital, he showed me a picture of a little boy with his head in the jaws of a giant crocodile."

"How can this be?" Andreas wondered.

" 'We have learned to get along with each other,' he said. 'Crocodiles are tame in my country.'

"I laughed and asked, 'How can you live here in Dürnstein if you are afraid of the Danube?'

" 'I have to make a living,' he replied."

"It's not a laughing matter, Savannah," Andreas said. "It's called potomophobia, fear of rivers or running water."

"That's a real phobia? How do you know these things? Do you know everything?"

"Not everything. But it could have been hereditary or caused by a specific trigger event. I'm just glad you got here safely. Thank you for coming."

"Is there someone you want me to call? Your parents?"

"No." Andreas was adamant.

"Didn't you say your family lives in Vienna?"

"Don't involve my family. I don't want them to worry. Promise me?"

Savannah threw up her hands. "I promise." What was Andreas hiding? Why didn't he want her to notify his family?

"Who could have done this to you? You don't think—"

Andreas had his suspicions but didn't think sharing them with Savannah was wise until he was certain of his conclusion.

He squeezed her hand. As long as he had that connection with Savannah, he felt safe. "We'll let the police sort it out. How long will I be in here?"

"The doctors say a few more days."

A nurse came in and checked his vital signs. Then she administered a shot.

"Mrs. Bauer, he's looking much better this morning."

Andreas's eyebrows raised.

Savannah leaned in and whispered, "I had to tell them I was your wife or they wouldn't have let me near you."

Andreas smiled. "Mrs. Bauer. I like the sound of that." Then he closed his eyes.

"I gave him something for the pain," said the nurse. "It will help him sleep. He'll be out for several hours, if you want to take a break. You've hardly left his bedside."

"I'll stay, if you don't mind. I can catch up on my sleep on the sofa."

Savannah wanted to confront her uncle, but she was afraid to leave Andreas's side. It had been touch and go throughout the night, and she wanted to be here for him in case he needed her or, God forbid, he slipped away before she could say goodbye.

"Sleep, Andreas, my darling."

Chapter Sixteen

Saffron Fact: The ancient Persians used saffron to treat stomach problems, and mixed it into hot teas to treat melancholy.

"Where are you?"

"At the hospital."

"My God, what happened?"

"I can't really talk. You're not supposed to use cell phones here. Can I call you back?"

"No, you can't. I flew all the way from Charleston. I was worried sick about you. Malcolm didn't have any idea where you were. He said you didn't come home last night or the night before."

"I think Uncle Malcolm knows exactly where I am and why."

"What is that supposed to mean?"

Savannah tried to change the subject. "You're here, in Austria?"

"Yes, with Malcolm and Ilsa. I called your father, and he flew home early from his honeymoon with that waitress, Kiki."

"Cindi," Savannah corrected. "I'm sorry I worried everyone. My—my friend, Andreas, the one I told you about, is in the hospital. I don't want to leave him."

"Are you getting serious with this boy?"

"I think, yes. I'm falling in love with him." She

looked over at Andreas, and he was still asleep.

"Well, then, tell me where you are. I want to meet him."

"I don't think that's a good idea. I'll come back to the winery."

"Are you afraid I'll interrogate him?"

"Yes, I know you will, and he's in no condition to be questioned. The police were already here. He doesn't remember a thing. It's not a good time."

"The police? I am coming right over there. I'll have Malcolm drive me."

"No, I don't want him anywhere near Andreas. If you must come, come alone."

Savannah turned to Andreas. His eyelids fluttered.

"Are you awake?" she asked.

"Yes. I keep drifting off. Sorry. I'm terrible company."

"I wouldn't want to be anywhere else. But I have some bad news for you. My mother's coming over."

"Your mother, from Charleston?"

"Apparently, I forgot to tell anyone where I was, and I've been gone for two nights. Everyone is worried. My father had to cut his honeymoon short. Sorry."

"Why are you apologizing?"

"Because my mother is going to give you the third degree. And I'm sure she's already gotten an earful from Uncle Malcolm."

"I'm happy to meet her."

"You say that now. Dina is a lot like those hurricanes that blow into Charleston. The ones that leave a path of destruction in their wake. They seem calm, but that's just the eye of the storm, and then they come back more powerful than ever."

"That bad?"

"Worse than you can imagine."

Andreas laughed and then cringed. "It hurts when I laugh. I don't look like much."

"You look wonderful." She touched his unbandaged palm. "You're alive."

"And you look exhausted," Andreas said. "Your bow is off center."

"Well, I know you're improving if you notice my bow. And you're right. I'd better fix my hair before my mother gets here. I've worn this bow two days in a row. In her book, that's unacceptable."

"I want to make a good impression."

Savannah laughed. "There's not much of you to see behind all those bandages and wires. But I don't care what she thinks."

Andreas looked at Savannah adoringly. "I love you."

"Y-you do?"

"Of course. I knew the minute I saw you I was going to love you for the rest of my life. I don't want you to go back to Scotland or to Charleston. I want you to stay right here, with me. I want to marry you. I'd get down on one knee if I could. And I don't have a ring. And I don't have a winery or a bow business, but everything I do have is yours."

Savannah's eyes started tearing. "Oh, Andreas. I love you, too."

"Is that a yes?"

Savannah smiled and leaned over to kiss Andreas on the forehead. "I think you're delirious. It's probably the pain medication talking. I won't hold you to it."

"Is that a yes?" he repeated.

"We'll talk about it later."

"I want to talk about it now," Andreas insisted, frowning. "Will you marry me?"

Savannah smiled. "Yes, but it's not official until you walk out of this hospital."

"That's wonderful. I want to call my parents and sisters and tell them the good news, but I can't get out of bed. I don't want them to worry, so we'll take a trip to Vienna as soon as I'm better and tell them in person."

Savannah reached for Andreas's hand. "I can't wait to meet them."

Savannah's mother flew into the room and gathered her daughter in her arms.

"Savannah Sutherland, you had us scared to death. Don't ever do that again."

"Sorry, Mother. How did you get in? They're only allowing family."

"I'm your family. And did you ever know anyone who could refuse your mother?"

"Well, no." Savannah turned to Andreas. "Mother, this is Andreas Bauer."

Dina moved closer to inspect the patient.

"Can't see the man under all those bandages. I'm sure you're in there somewhere. I'm Savannah's mother Dina. I'd shake your hand, if I could find it."

Andreas blinked. He found himself face to face with one of the most glamorous women he'd ever seen. Savannah was the image of her mother. She couldn't possibly be Savannah's mother. A sister, maybe. Unless she had Savannah when she was a teenager. And she was wearing a bow sprinkled with what looked like diamonds that brought out the sparkle in her green eyes.

Savannah's eyes.

"Well, aren't you going to say anything?"

"I—I'm pleased to meet you, Dina," Andreas stuttered.

"What are you staring at?"

"It's just that, well, it's obvious where Savannah gets her good looks. But you don't look like anybody's mother."

Dina flashed him a high-wattage smile. "Maybe there's something to this boy after all. I was a child bride."

Savannah shook her head. "You want to know why I don't have any lasting relationships? They take one look at my mother, and I'm rendered invisible."

"Savannah has a tendency to exaggerate."

"Well you can't have this one, Mother. Andreas and I are engaged."

"Engaged! Since when?"

"Since a moment ago."

"What about the handsome man your uncle said—"

"You met Lukas?"

"Yes. He was at the house. We were all worried about you. He was quite taken with my bow."

Savannah sighed. "Lukas is a wolf, Mother."

"I'll say. He hit on me."

"Well, you're welcome to him."

"Your uncle seems to think you two were getting serious."

"Uncle Malcolm is serious about acquiring Lukas's family winery and annexing the adjacent property."

"I love your daughter, Mrs. Sutherland," Andreas said.

"I'm not Mrs. Anybody, young man. And love

doesn't pay the rent. Malcolm says you're a poor saffron farmer. How are you going to support my daughter?"

"Andreas is a distinguished botanist," Savannah argued.

"There's money to be made in the saffron business, and I can definitely support Savannah. It might take me awhile to establish myself."

"Mother, I don't care if Andreas has no money. I'm in love with him. He is the man I'm going to marry."

"And you're going to live in Scotland in the Deep Freeze?"

"No, we're going to live right here in Austria."

"And what about your legacy?"

"Mother, I've already told you I'm not interested in running your business."

Dina glared at her daughter. "Then what do you plan to do with your life?"

Savannah had wondered the same thing for years. She thought putting her degree in Sustainability to use was a viable option. And, in her mind, working at Uncle Malcolm's winery might provide that opportunity.

"Uncle Malcolm wants me to take over Kleppinger's, but I never understood why."

"Because he has no one to leave it to. He and Ilsa never had children."

"And Daddy would love me to work at Glenn Castle Inn."

"As a waitress like Trixi?"

"It's Cindi."

"I've worked my whole life to build my business, and I want you to run it one day."

"Mother, that's *your* business. Your dream, not mine."

"So what do you plan to do with your degree in Sustainability?"

"My degree fits perfectly with Andreas's organic saffron business."

"We're not through talking about this, young lady. I have some things to say to you. But now you need to get some rest. Let me take you back to your uncle's."

"I'm not going back there, but we can talk in the waiting room so Andreas can sleep. I'm not going to leave him. You and I need to talk. I have a wedding to plan."

"I hope Andreas doesn't have opinions about the wedding."

"I'm sure he'll want to have a say."

"What groom cares about his wedding?"

"I'll have to ask him. We haven't discussed any details. But it's not your wedding."

"It most certainly is," Dina disagreed, turning on her heels and sashaying out the door.

"If you're listening, I'm sorry she was so rude to you," Savannah apologized.

"That's okay. I understand she only wants the best for you."

"And you are the best," Savannah said. "At any rate, you're stuck with me. I'm not going back to my uncle's, so you have yourself a roommate."

Andreas reached for Savannah's hand. "Don't hide your light behind your mother."

"I didn't know I was doing that."

"You seem quieter when she's around."

"She's like the sun. When she's in a room,

everything else is in shadow."

"And you are like a shining star. My shining star."

Savannah smiled.

A nurse came in and announced, "Visiting hours are over. I'm going to give Herr Bauer a sedative so he can sleep and heal."

Savannah bent over and kissed Andreas lightly on his bruised lips, releasing his hand. He grimaced. She told him, "I'll be right outside, waiting here when you wake up. Now get some sleep."

"One thing," Andreas whispered. "I love you." He smiled widely, then grunted in pain.

The night nurse administered the drugs, and Andreas's eyes rolled back in his head.

Savannah picked up her handbag and led her mother to the empty waiting room. She took the couch and her mother settled into a nearby armchair.

"Would you like some coffee, Mother?"

"No, I'm fine. I had some at Malcolm and Ilsa's, but I'm going to move to a hotel."

"Why? They have plenty of room, and I won't be going back there."

"Why ever not?"

"I just don't feel comfortable there. I think Uncle Malcolm might have had something to do with putting Andreas into the hospital."

Dina's eyes widened. "You really believe that?"

"Uncle Malcolm has been against my relationship with Andreas from the start. He wouldn't let Andreas have the land he needs to start his saffron business. And he's intent on marrying me off to Lukas Baeder."

"Would that really be so terrible?"

"Mom, I don't love Lukas Baeder. He's nice to

look at, and on the surface he appears to be a gentleman. But he's a predator. He's a smooth talker, but I get the feeling he wants to talk me out of my clothes. He's just his father's agent. He wants me because it will give him access to Kleppinger's. In his mind, I'm the Holy Grail."

Dina looked away and a tear slipped down her face.

"Mother, what's wrong?"

Dina heaved a heavy sigh. "Darling, I have the feeling that history is repeating itself."

"What do you mean?"

"Two fine men. One woman. It's a long story."

"I'm not going anywhere."

The air-conditioning unit cycled on, and for a moment Dina looked up at the ceiling, hoping to put off the inevitable conversation. The circular nurse's station in the center of the room was lit up but the hallway light was dim. Dina's eyes were focused on a fire extinguisher at the back of the room. Her memories were already rooted in another place and time.

Chapter Seventeen

Saffron Fact: You only need a few strands of saffron to flavor an entire meal. Using too many strands gives you a bitter flavor.

"I wasn't much more than a girl myself, younger than you, but I thought I was so worldly," began Dina with a wan smile. "My mother sent me on a trip to Europe after college graduation. I went with a friend, who met a boy and decided to stay in Italy, so I was on my own when I flew to Scotland, the next leg of our itinerary.

"We were booked to stay at Glenn Castle Inn, and honestly, it was the most beautiful place in the world. That's where I met Connor Sutherland. He was working there over the summer, and the moment I saw him, that was it for me. He was a big, handsome Scotsman with a sexy accent, and I was fixated on what was under his kilt. Turns out it's true that they wear nothing under those things."

"Mother!"

"I'm just trying to tell you how it was for me, for us. How do you think you were conceived? It was cold, even in the summer, and he was as attracted to me as I was to him. I would sit by the fire and read, and he would keep me company, and we would snuggle up to keep warm. He spent every moment he wasn't at work with me. I fell so hard, I canceled the rest of my trip and spent the time with Connor in Scotland.

"Connor went home and told his father about me. He was so excited. 'I found a girl, Da. She's the one.' Well, he asked me to marry him, and I knew my parents wouldn't approve, so I accepted and we had a hasty wedding at the hotel. I was a virgin, and we couldn't wait to be together. It was a small ceremony. His father, Ian, was there, and his mother and his twin brother—his *identical* twin brother, Malcolm—was there, too. It was the happiest time in my life.

"Well, things went smoothly for about a year. But Connor was working all the time. He was trying to become manager of the Inn, and that required a lot of overtime. He said he was doing it for us, for the family he wanted to have with me, but we rarely saw each other. I barely survived that first winter. It was freezing, and when it wasn't cold it was raining or snowing, and I was cooped up in his parents' house with no one to talk to. We had a room there because Connor couldn't afford a house on his salary. I began to regret my decision. I felt trapped. I had a college degree in business I wasn't using, and I felt I was wasting my life. Connor didn't have high aspirations. His dream was to be a manager at Glenn Castle Inn. He wanted a big family, but he couldn't afford it. But he wanted a child so much, I agreed. We tried, but I couldn't seem to get pregnant. Nothing was working out."

Dina rubbed her eyes with the back of her hand.

Savannah reached over and patted her mother's hand. "Go on."

"Meanwhile, Connor's brother, Malcolm, was always available and always around. When Connor first brought me home, Malcolm acted sullen, always brooding whenever he was there. I thought he didn't like me. It was only later that I realized why he was that way. When he walked by, he would *accidentally* brush my arm and cause my pulse to race. Or he'd pull back my hair and plant a soft, wet kiss on my neck. Every time we were together, he'd greet me with an innocent kiss, meant for the cheek, but it inevitably found its way to my lips and lingered there. He was a merciless flirter. He made it clear he wanted me. I knew he was—we were—treading on dangerous ground.

" 'You married the wrong brother,' he whispered once, pulling me close when no one was looking.

It was Malcolm who gave me the idea for my bow business. One day he came home with a piece of plaid ribbon. He massaged my scalp, then tied the ribbon around my head and fashioned it into a bow. He took both of my hands in his and said, 'Now I will think of you wearing this ribbon and nothing else.' I knew it was inappropriate, but that didn't stop me from responding to him or daydreaming about him whenever I was alone, which was often. I was so lonely.

"Then, one night, Connor called and said he would be working late, again. I was furious. I had prepared an intimate dinner and drinks, but he wasn't coming home. It was our one-year anniversary. I had one drink and then another, and another. I skipped dinner, got into a new negligee, and fell asleep. Connor's parents were at a party. I was alone again. Then I heard the door open, and Connor tiptoed in, locking the door behind him.

" 'Darling, did I wake you?' he whispered.

" 'Connor, you're home,' I cried and welcomed him with open arms. He kissed me on my neck and worked his way up to my lips, lapping me up like a hungry tiger. That night, when we made love, it was like a revelation, maybe because it was dark and I was drunk and it had been so long since we'd last made love. He was more amorous than usual, the way he slowly slipped off my nightgown and kissed every part of my body, in places his mouth had never been, starting with my breasts. Connor had never done that before. It was like he was a different man. My body was on fire, and the things he did to me that night and the things I did to him, these were things Connor and I had never tried. I had multiple orgasms. That had never happened, especially not when my husband was inside of me."

"Mother!"

"Do you want to hear the story or not?"

"Sorry. I do. Go on."

"We couldn't get enough of each other. It was like we were making love for the first time. He was so excited. He kept saying he loved me and touched me like he was touching me for the first time. I had never felt so cherished, so satisfied. The last thing I remember before we were interrupted was Connor massaging my scalp and kissing my neck, his lips lingering seductively.

"Then, suddenly, the door splintered and the lights came on, blinding me. I stiffened. To go from such pleasure to such pain in a moment's time was jarring. I could see the contempt in your grandfather Ian's eyes. Connor's father dragged him from on top of me like he weighed nothing at all. Connor was a big man, but his father was a giant. I was completely naked. I pulled the covers up over me in embarrassment.

" 'Da,' Connor cried, sullen and brooding. 'For Christ's sake!'

" 'What's going on?' I screamed.

" 'That's what I'd like to know. Connor called me. His car's broken down. He said he tried to reach you both, but you weren't answering your phones. He told me he left work early to surprise you, Dina. He was promoted to manager, and he wanted to celebrate. He got someone else to work his shift. I came away from the party to get him and left him waiting for a tow. When I got home and saw Malcolm's car but couldn't find Mal, I passed by Connor's room and heard voices. I tried your door, but it was locked. Looks like I'm the one who got a surprise. He's on his way home now, Mal, so you'd better get your boaby out of your brother's wife. You always wanted what your brother had. And I guess you found a way to take it. But this time you've crossed the line. Do you really hate him that much?'

" 'Da, I love my brother,' he said, starting to get dressed, adding, 'but I'm in love with Dina.'

"Ian slapped him and nearly knocked him off his feet. 'That makes it all right, then, does it? In love? Do you even know the meaning of the word? How could you disrespect your brother this way? I've a mind to tell him, but it would break his heart.'

"I couldn't believe this was happening. My heart stopped.

" 'Malcolm?' I was suddenly wide awake. 'Malcolm? I thought—'

" 'I'm sorry, Dina. It was the only way I could have you.'

"Ian turned to me. 'You'll need to leave, lass. I'll

no' have you coming between my boys. Get out of my sight. Malcolm Craig Sutherland, you're coming with me.'

"I screamed when I realized what I had done. I was horrified. 'What am I going to tell Connor?'

" 'I don't give a damn as long as you're gone before he gets home,' Ian said. 'I'll pack up your things and send them to you. I want you out of my house, tonight.'

"So I had to flee the house like a criminal, leave my things, leave my marriage, in the dead of night. The thought of leaving Connor all alone with no explanation was unthinkable. He was a good man, and I hated hurting him. He would never understand.

"Looking back on that night, I think I should have realized that it wasn't Connor in my bed. Malcolm and Connor were identical twins, but I was Connor's wife. How could I not have known my own husband's body? How could I make love with a stranger? And enjoy it so much? I blamed myself. I was so ashamed. But I didn't regret it, because I have you, Savannah. I left a note, giving Connor some weak excuse and asking for a divorce before I flew back to Charleston."

Savannah sagged and clutched her stomach. "You slept with Uncle Malcolm? You cheated on my father with his own brother?"

"No, it wasn't intentional. I thought he was your father."

"I don't believe it."

"Your grandmother was furious when I got home," Dina continued. "She took me back, but she never let me forget her earlier warnings."

"Did you speak to Da again after that?"

"Connor flew over. He pleaded with me to come back. He never stopped trying. He never gave up. Meanwhile, I wanted to leave Charleston, to leave with Connor, but that was impossible. Soon after I arrived home, I found out I was pregnant. I had no savings, no job. I had no choice. That's when I became determined to make money of my own. So I started Southern Signature Accessories and worked hard to make it a success so we'd never have to depend on anyone else again.

"And then Malcolm called to apologize, and my mother answered the phone and told him I was pregnant, thinking it was Connor. He offered to marry me. But how could I ever go back there? He told his father, and his father's lawyer called. That's when I agreed to send you to Scotland every summer. Before you were old enough to fly by yourself, Ian came over and got you at the beginning of each summer and brought you back home in September. But he couldn't look me in the eye. He said if I didn't agree to his terms, he'd tell Connor the truth. And I could not hurt him that way. Poor Connor was alone his whole life, until he met Barbi."

"Cindi."

"And she really makes him happy?"

"She seems to."

"I was glad he had you in his life."

"Did you ever love my father?"

"Of course I did. When he called to tell me he was marrying that waitress, I told him 'If we weren't already divorced, I'd divorce you again.' But how could I blame your father? I left him."

"Why didn't you ever tell me this before?"

"Because I hoped you'd never find out. But now, now that Mal wants you to inherit his property, I thought you should know why."

"Because he slept with you once?"

"Because he's your father."

Savannah jumped out of her seat and faced her mother menacingly.

"Take that back."

"I'm sorry, but I thought you deserved the truth."

"How can you be so sure?"

"Because I hadn't slept with Connor for weeks before that night. He was always so tired when he came home, too tired to make love. The truth is, he left me long before I left him."

"Mom, how could you know that?"

"A woman knows."

"But you're not sure."

"Not definitely. You're a Sutherland. That's all that matters."

"Connor Sutherland will always be my father," Savannah said stubbornly.

"He's a fine man."

Savannah hugged her shoulders and stretched. "Now it all makes sense. Why Uncle Malcolm wants to leave me the winery. He thinks I'm his daughter."

"You could be. You most probably are."

"Why didn't you marry Uncle Malcolm?"

"Well, that's a long story—actually it's your Grandpa Ian's story. Your grandfather was a war hero, did you know that?"

"You never talked much about him."

"Well, we didn't get along at the end, but that doesn't take anything away from the kind of man he was. He was a member of the Highland infantry regiment of the British Army—the Sutherland Highlanders—during World War II. They have a long, proud history since 1881—The Black Watch, The Argyll and Southern Highlanders, The Cameronians, The Gordon Highlanders, The Seaforths. They had fifteen battalions during the First World War and nine during the Second World War.

"In the Great War, they called the Black Watch "devils in skirts" and the "ladies from hell." Sometimes English regiments in the trenches would shout out that they were the Black Watch, to demoralize the Germans. The Fighting Highlanders were known for bravery in the face of the enemy. They fought in France, North Africa, Sicily, the Normandy landings, and campaigns through France and into Germany. The regiments hold a special place in the hearts of the Scottish people. It's part of the reason pipers play at Scots weddings."

"What happened to Grandpa during the war?" Savannah asked. "He never talked about it much."

"I think that's true of a lot of people who fought in the war. Did you know Ian's parents were both killed during Scotland's Blitz?"

"I thought 'the Blitz' were air raids on London."

"Scotland was attacked in Glasgow, Clydebank, Edinburgh, Aberdeen, and Dundee."

"Why did they bomb Scotland?"

"The factories, coal mines, engineering works, and shipyards were important targets for German bombers because they were crucial to the war effort. German planes flew across the North Sea to drop bombs on Scotland. Hundreds of people were killed, injured, or left homeless. In Clydebank alone, forty thousand people were made homeless. It's hard for us to understand because in America our home front was safe.

"At Dunkirk in 1940, the Scots regiments held the Germans long enough for the British army to be evacuated from the French beaches. The 1st Royal Scots from Edinburgh were virtually wiped out. After Dunkirk, Churchill abandoned the Highlanders at St. Valéry. The story is that Churchill attempted a landing to rescue them, but weather moved in and prevented it. In any case, the 51st Highland Division was forced to surrender. That left almost every family in the highlands affected. They surrendered at the town of St. Valéry-En-Caux to German Field Marshal Rommel."

"I thought Rommel was in Egypt."

"That was later. He was at El Alamein in Egypt in 1942. There the reconstituted 51st Highland Division, along with the Australian and New Zealand divisions, fought under Major General Wimberley, known as Tartan Tam because he insisted that his division wear the kilt. They fought through sandstorms and explosives, their kilts flying and bagpipes playing. They defeated Field Marshal Rommel in that battle that turned the tide of war against the Germans."

"And I thought they got all of the soldiers out at Dunkirk."

"Well, of course you always hear about the military successes. But what followed right after Dunkirk was one of the worst modern military disasters to befall Scottish soldiers. They did evacuate a large part of the British Army, but almost two weeks later, the Scots regiments had to pay the price. Some ten thousand of the survivors—the original 51st Highland Division—

went into captivity in Germany for the remainder of the war."

Savannah shook her head and took a seat on the couch. "I never knew that."

"It's not something you hear much about outside of Scotland. But the Scots prisoners found a way to communicate back to Scotland. Shortly after those soldiers arrived at their POW camp, they devised a dance known as The Reel of the 51st Division. When two British privates of the Argyll and Sutherland Highlanders escaped, they took the steps back to Scotland, where the reel became popular. It was danced to show solidarity with the imprisoned Highland soldiers. It's still danced to this day.

"Finally, after the D-day landings in 1944, the 51st liberated St. Valéry, parading through the street with pipes and drums."

"I do remember Grandpa Ian taking me to a war memorial before he died. So what did Grandpa Ian's story during the war have to do with you and Uncle Malcolm?"

"You look absolutely worn out, honey. Why don't you rest on the couch and we'll talk tomorrow."

"I want to hear about it now," Savannah said, struggling to stay awake.

Dina blew out a breath. "Well, lie back on the couch and close your eyes. I suppose this story needed to come out."

Marilyn Baron

Part Two
Ian's Story

Marilyn Baron

Chapter Eighteen

Saffron Fact: In ancient times, saffron was known as the "queen of plants."

"Dina."

"Malcolm." Clutching the phone, hearing his voice, she couldn't help but think of that first, last, and only night she and Mal were together, in Connor's bed in his childhood room at the Sutherlands' family home. Her life had changed so drastically since that night. A night she would never forget. She played it over and over again in her mind, like a videotape unspooling.

"How are you? How is Savannah?"

"We're fine. How's Connor?"

"Still pining away for you."

"That's not funny."

"If only I had met you first, I would have made you mine. When my brother brought you home I was so jealous, I couldn't see straight. I knew you were the one for me."

There was no good response to that statement.

"Look, Dina. I called because I have some news."

Dina remained silent.

"I'm getting married."

Dina bit her lip until it bled.

"Dina, are you there?"

"It didn't take you long to get over me."

"I didn't have a choice. Right after, after we—"

"After you—"

"I take full responsibility," Malcolm asserted, pausing. "Do you ever think of that night?"

She denied it. But she was lying. Her cheeks burned at the thought of what she'd let him do to her body that night. No man since had ever come close to the reaction she'd had to Malcolm Sutherland's touch. If Ian hadn't pulled Malcolm out of her bed, she knew they would have continued their affair, behind his brother's back. She was helpless in the face of their newfound passion. One night wouldn't have been enough for either of them.

"Dina?"

Malcolm took Dina's continued silence as permission to continue.

"As soon as he found us together, Da dragged me off to a little town in Austria—Dürnstein. Why that town? I wondered. When he was talking to me again, when he got over his mad, Da told me a story about his time as a prisoner of war after Dunkirk…"

****

He was held in Stalag 17B, near Krems, with a population of about thirty thousand, primarily U.S. airmen. It was a brutal experience. The men lived under horrific conditions. Each compound was designed for a hundred and forty men, but sometimes they crammed in as many as four thousand. The camp was surrounded by electrified fences and gun towers. The men were forced to endure appalling hardships. They were starved. Men were bayoneted and shot for the most minor infractions. And it was very arbitrary. They never knew what was coming.

126

The only reason he survived was because of a certain senior officer in the camp, Johannes Kleppinger, whose family was very wealthy and owned a winery nearby in Dürnstein. He was very humane. Ian, as an officer, received better treatment because of his rank. Kleppinger used to sneak extra food to the prisoners whenever he could. He never said anything, but by his actions, Ian could tell he didn't agree with Hitler's thuggish tactics. When his family needed to harvest the grapes, he arranged for a group of prisoners to be transported in a work convoy to the Kleppinger estate just seven kilometers from the camp.

There was a group of them in the van. They had almost made it away from the camp when a prison guard stopped the truck. A hotshot Cajun pilot named Bastian LaBontay was driving. Kleppinger was in the passenger seat. LaBontay was a favorite among the men, though he wasn't a Highlander. He was something of a rebel and a misfit and had gotten separated from his men. A braver soul there never was, so the Highlanders "adopted" him and lovingly called him "Bonnie." He tolerated that from his friends but wouldn't allow anyone else to use that moniker.

"*Halt*," the guard barked in German. "*Namen*."

"Stop the car and give him your name," said Kleppinger.

"Bastian LaBontay," he answered.

"Bastard?" the guard asked, laughing.

The men in the car froze. Bonnie's temper was legendary, and he had already suffered enough indignities at the hands of the Germans. He was at his limit. His friends had saved him countless times by talking him down, even holding him down when he threatened to explode. His temper had been pushed to the breaking point. Somehow, he had managed to stay under the radar.

"Bonnie," admonished Kleppinger in a whisper.

But the guard had heard it.

"Did you say 'Bonnie'?" he teased.

"Bastian LaBontay," sounded Bonnie clearly.

Bonnie's first, brief whiff of freedom had emboldened him. He was so close to escaping his nightmare he could taste it. He was through being ordered around.

"Bonnie? Where's Clyde?" The guard laughed hysterically.

Bonnie's hands tightened on the wheel. "The next Kraut that calls me that gets two between the eyes."

"*Scheisse*." Kleppinger shook his head.

"Bonnie and Clyde. Bonnie and Clyde." The guard repeated relentlessly in a sing-song voice.

The inevitable happened before anyone could stop it, seemingly in slow motion. Bonnie reached across and grabbed the gun from Kleppinger's holster. He aimed the weapon at the guard, his hands shaking.

"Fuck, Bonnie, what are you doing?" Ian pleaded from the back seat.

But it was too late. The guard put two bullets between Bonnie's eyes, and blood spattered everywhere. Bonnie slid down in his seat,.

"*Verdammt*," Kleppinger yelled. "We have papers, you idiot."

"All of you. Out of the car." The guard waved his gun menacingly.

"*Arschloch*," Kleppinger seethed. Followed by a resounding round of "shits" in various languages and dialects.

The men got out of the car. They were of the same mind. These Fighting Highlanders were going to leave this hellhole that moment or die trying.

Kleppinger confronted the guard, waving his papers. "I'm taking these men to my winery to pick grapes. I have the proper permissions."

"I'm taking you all in," the guard argued.

A battle cry rang out, and all the men, with the exception of a very bewildered Johannes Kleppinger, charged the guard and started beating on him.

"This one's for Bonnie," yelled Ian.

"For Bonnie," said another, taking up the cry.

Venting their anger and the humiliations they'd suffered during their long confinement, they pounded on the German, individually and collectively, until he was unconscious.

Kleppinger grabbed the officer's gun, aimed, and shot the guard between his eyes. The men stood in amazement.

"That went well," Kleppinger stated, wiping the sweat from his brow.

Ian looked up, incredulous. "You shot him."

"He was half-dead already. If he regained consciousness, we'd all be paying for it."

"What are you going to do?" Ian addressed the German officer.

"Get him the hell out of here. Come on. Throw his body in the back. We'll dump it in the Danube on the way. We'll bury Bonnie at my home."

Kleppinger sat in a pool of Bonnie's blood in the driver's seat. Ian cradled Bonnie's head in the back seat. Bonnie's blood leached onto his prison uniform.

The men chanted a Scottish prayer and sang quiet mourning songs.

Kleppinger gunned the motor and set out for his family estate.

"We can't ever go back," he said. To a man, they understood and swore a vow of silence.

****

"Da said Bonnie saved him, and Kleppinger did too. They worked hard on the vineyard, but they got proper food and lodging. Some of the men even escaped back to Scotland. Kleppinger just let them go and never reported them. Whenever he could, Kleppinger requisitioned more prisoners for work duty, explaining that some of his workers had died due to harsh conditions at the vineyard. By the time they were liberated, all of the prisoners were malnourished except the working crew Johannes Kleppinger was able to protect. He prevented a lot of deaths. A lot of men, including my father, owe their lives to this man.

"They still tend Bonnie's grave and place fresh flowers," said Malcolm reverently. "There's a lovely headstone to mark his resting place.

"Da and Johannes Kleppinger kept up a correspondence after the war. So Da took me there to meet the man and have him knock some sense into me, give me a job, keep me away from my brother. And my brother's wife. He told me not to come home.

"Well, Johannes Kleppinger put me to work in the vineyard like he had my father. He had a daughter, younger than me, but easy on the eyes. Faced with not being able to have you or to go home again while my father is still alive, I've made the best of it. Her name is Ilsa.

"She's very sweet, and pliable. She fell in love with me."

"You seduced her."

"Yes, but I did grow to love her. She persuaded her father to accept the union. Da, Ma, and Connor will come to the wedding, but I can't go back to Scotland, at least not until my Da is buried. Connor will never understand it. I can't tell him. So he's not only lost you, he's lost me too, and he'll never know why.

"I promised Da I would not contact you, but I wanted you to know. I'm sorry for what I did to Connor, and to you. But I'm not sorry for that night. I was in love with you. I still am."

"So you're going to marry someone else, after you ruined my life. How very noble."

"If I could take it back—"

"So I'm glad everything worked out for you. You will inherit a vineyard, and your brother will be working at that damned Inn for the rest of his life, lonely and unhappy."

"You wouldn't have been happy with my brother. You deserve more. He was married to his job."

"But that was my decision to make. Now I'm alone."

"You have Savannah."

"And Savannah will grow up not knowing her father."

"Da will never let that happen. Did he—"

"His lawyer contacted me. I've agreed to sign the papers."

"I hope I get to meet her one day."

"You're not her father."

"Did you have a paternity test done?"

"I don't need to have a test done. Besides, you're identical twins. I'm not sure a test would tell us anything definitively."

"I'll make sure she's taken care of."

"Connor is paying child support. I think you've done enough."

"Will you send pictures?"

"I'll send pictures to her father."

Then she hung up on him.

****

"After Grandpa died, Uncle Malcolm spent a lot of time at the house when I was there every summer," Savannah reported.

"How did the brothers get along?"

"Da was happy to have Uncle Malcolm home. I'm glad you told me. It explains a lot about why the brothers were so estranged for so long."

"It wasn't an easy thing to admit."

Savannah took her mother's hand.

By the time Andreas was released from the hospital later that week, Savannah had rarely left his side. In fact, the doctor only agreed to sign the discharge papers because she confirmed she wouldn't leave him unattended. When he was cleared to leave the hospital, Savannah took Andreas in a taxi and settled him into his house at the railway station.

Andreas was not a very good patient.

"I want to check on the plants," he said, as she helped him gingerly out of the cab.

"There's plenty of time for that," Savannah admonished. "I've set up a bed for you on the couch downstairs, since you won't be able to make it to your bedroom for a while. It's my job to make sure you follow all of the doctor's instructions."

He frowned. "What about—?"

"We won't be able to do that for a while either. You need to take it easy."

"Will you go back to your uncle's?"

"Not until we find out who put you in the hospital. Whoever it is, I'm not going to leave you until you're recovered. You need someone to fix your meals. And who's going to take care of your saffron garden? And what if whoever attacked you comes back again to finish the job? Besides, you need to be better before you can handle the excursions from the riverboats. We need to set up your classroom, work on your presentations, and prepare the kitchen to produce the saffron products."

"I never asked if you could cook."

"I'm afraid I take after my mother in that department. Our specialty is making reservations."

Andreas reached out for Savannah's hand. "I don't know how to thank you. If you weren't here, I don't know what I'd do. I would truly be lost."

"You'd find a way. The police came by the hospital while you were unconscious. They wanted to know if you remembered anything, but the nurse told them you weren't up to talking. They're going to come by this afternoon to ask you some questions about the incident."

"That's a rather benign way of referring to the attack. This wasn't just some random event. I was targeted, and they're never going to catch whoever did this to me."

"That's a defeatist attitude."

"I didn't see anything. They came up behind me. I

was incapacitated before I realized what was happening."

"Well, they dusted for fingerprints, so we'll see if anything comes up."

"Do you really think your uncle had something to do with this?"

"You know he was against you buying some of his land. He wants to seal the deal with Lukas's family to merge the two vineyards, and my involvement with you ruins his plans. I hope he wouldn't resort to violence. Maybe it was Lukas. Or he had Lukas help him. Whoever did it, they almost killed you."

"Don't remind me."

"If it was my uncle, they won't come back while I'm here. And I'm not going to leave you."

Savannah sat across from him on a wing chair. "Maybe someone was just trying to put the fear of God into you. Who else could have done this to you?"

Andreas scratched his head. "The fear of God. Hmm. I met with Father Abbot at the Melk Abbey right before I was beaten."

"Are you saying the Reverend Father could have sent thugs to beat you up?"

"I found something in those saffron manuals, something that implicates the monastery in a major theft."

"Something bad enough to have you killed?"

"The less you know about it, the better. But if what I discovered is true, then yes, they'll want to bury it and me with it."

"Are you going to tell the police?"

"The Abbey is so well connected, I don't think they can be touched."

"Do you have proof?"

"Only my notes. I hand-copied the manuals. Actually, I have a lot of it on my cell phone, too, even though photography isn't allowed in the libraries. If not for that, I'd still be in that library, hand-copying notes. It's only speculation, but the Reverend Father issued veiled threats. But it would be his word against mine. I plan to confront him."

"Andreas, do you think that's a wise idea? The church is very powerful. Maybe we should just drop the whole thing and hope whoever did this doesn't return."

"I prefer to take a more aggressive approach. I have to live here, so I need to get to the bottom of this. And I need to protect my family." Andreas looked into Savannah's eyes. I haven't forgotten, you know."

"Forgotten what?"

"That you agreed to marry me. So this is our home, and I am going to protect you."

"I'm perfectly capable of protecting myself. We can protect each other. What do you have in mind?"

"I don't know yet. I'll be able to think better as soon as my head stops hurting."

Savannah got up from the chair, leaned over, and kissed his bandage gently. "I'm sorry."

"Lower," he whispered.

"Lower?"

"Kiss me properly. On the lips."

She obliged.

"Ouch."

"That still hurts?"

"Every part of me still hurts, but your kiss just made it better." Andreas smiled. "Well, there's one part of me that doesn't hurt. Can you go a little lower?"

Savannah's eyes widened. "Remember, doctor's orders."

"I don't see the doctor anywhere around here, do you?"

Savannah waggled her finger at Andreas. "You're a devil. I'm not falling for that."

"You'd make a good nurse." He cocked his head and focused on Savannah's bow. The part of him that didn't hurt tightened. "Is that the Swiss flag you're wearing, or the Red Cross logo?"

"A bow for every occasion. My mother brought me a change of clothes and a new supply of bows."

"Lovely. But then, you look beautiful no matter what you have on…or off."

"Andreas." Savannah blushed and crinkled her nose. When Andreas talked like that, she was never offended. Lukas's crude bantering was another story. "Are you hungry?"

"I could eat, but there's nothing in the house."

"I'll go shopping. I could make you something simple. I can open up a can of soup, or how about some peanut butter-and-jelly sandwiches?"

"Ummm. A bowl of soup would be great. Thank you."

"Coming right up. I need to learn my way around the kitchen anyway."

"You already know your way around the bedroom."

"Andreas Bauer, behave yourself, or you'll end up in the doghouse."

"We don't have a doghouse."

"You know what I mean."

"Could you check on the plants?"

"Yes, let me go out now. But when I was here earlier, they hadn't come up yet."

"Thanks."

"We have an expression in the States: 'A watched pot never boils.' It's not going to do you any good to watch and wait for your plants to come up. They'll come up when they're ready to come up."

Nevertheless, Savannah went to the front yard to check on the garden. The soil hadn't been disturbed, and the plants weren't up yet. She reported her findings to Andreas.

"Sorry, but I'll check again tomorrow. I wish I had better news to report."

Two Months Later
Chapter Nineteen

Saffron Fact: Today, the latest research from Italy focuses on saffron benefits for optical health.

"Savannah, come quickly!"

Savannah flew through the door and skidded onto the patio.

Andreas was on his hands and knees.

"What's wrong?" she called. "Have they come back? Did you fall?"

"Nothing is wrong," Andreas said. "Everything is right. Look."

Savannah's eyes followed his, and as she drew in a breath her hand flew to her heart.

"Andreas, they're absolutely gorgeous," she marveled. "Oh, just look at them! The colors are so vibrant—purple, yellow, red. They're perfect."

"Our first blooms. Saffron season has started. This is the best time to collect them, when they've fully opened, right around mid-morning on a sunny day. You want to pick the flowers the first day they open when they're in full bloom."

"Aren't you going to use gloves?"

"No, just bare hands. The saffron threads are very delicate. We just pluck the stigmas from the flowers with our fingers. Don't pull the leaves, because it may harm the corms below the ground and destroy future growth. The plant can keep growing throughout the fall before the first hard freeze."

Andreas showed Savannah how to gather the flowers from the ground, pulling away the purple leaves and picking only the three willowy red threads or stigmas with his nails. He placed them delicately in a plastic container.

"Now we'll let them dry for a day or two in a warm place and then close the container to preserve them for cooking. So we'll have these to start baking and selling to cruise customers, and I want to bring some over to the restaurant in town that's agreed to cook saffron dishes. We have to harvest them right now. So come and help me collect them."

Savannah kneeled behind Andreas.

"Be careful of the bees. They like to rest on the flowers. Just swipe your hand and they'll fly off."

"This is so exciting. Can I touch them?"

"Of course. But be gentle."

"So all we save are the red-orange threads?"

"That's the valuable part—the three stigmas in the center of each of the saffron crocus flowers."

"How many plants will we have?"

"Remember, we planted about a hundred plants, but we'll grow them on a larger scale when I can acquire some additional land. We need to check the garden every day for new blooms. Then, each year, the corms, or bulbs, will multiply, and we'll be able to harvest more of the stigmas. After four to six years, we will divide and replant the corms after the foliage has faded.

"In a couple of days we'll be ready to make some of the products. I've got the recipes in the kitchen.

We'll need to shop for some of the ingredients. I think we should offer the saffron-infused chocolate and maybe the Gugelhupf cake on the excursions. And then we'll sell the raw saffron threads, some saffron salt, saffron honey, and some other products in the store."

"How do we cook with saffron?" Savannah inquired.

"To use the saffron, we'll steep the threads in hot liquid—water, broth, or milk, depending on the recipe—for about twenty minutes. Add both the threads and the steeping liquid early in the cooking or baking process, and the threads will continue to release their color and flavor."

"Are you ready with your presentation?"

"I think so. I could talk for hours on the subject. And I've had nothing else to do while I've been in confinement. You're a tough taskmaster."

"Sorry," Savannah said. "Your guests are going to love it."

"Does your mother want to come to our first session?" Andreas asked.

"I think she will. I'd love her to see the flowers in bloom. It might inspire her to create a saffron bow. I'm so glad she's decided to stay in town for a while. Since we've already set a date she'll want to stay for the wedding. She was staying at a hotel but now she's staying with Uncle Malcolm and Aunt Ilsa, but that's kind of awkward."

"Why?"

"Well, it's a long story, but once you hear it, you'll understand."

"I'm glad your father could arrange to have the wedding at Glenn Castle Inn."

"Yes, he's happy to do it. I'm looking forward to seeing him, to catch up and find out how the honeymoon went."

"I don't know what his new wife looks like, but I can't imagine how he let a woman as beautiful as your mother get away."

"Hmm."

"What does 'hmm' mean?"

"It's part of the long story. After the wedding, she'll want to fly back to America. She won't want to stay in Scotland. Too many painful memories. But she's been furiously working on our wedding plans."

"I can't wait to make you my bride. I may not be Scottish, but I'll even wear a kilt, so you'll get your dream wedding."

"What will you wear under the kilt?" Savannah teased.

"Savannah, you're a naughty girl. You'll find out on our wedding night."

"You don't need to wear a kilt. Da and Uncle Malcolm will have that covered."

"Or uncovered, as the case may be."

Chapter Twenty

Saffron Fact: Saffron has been used historically to treat everything from heartache to hemorrhoids.

"Dina, I'd like to talk to you about Savannah."

Dina stiffened and faced Malcolm. It was still difficult to be around the man. But he insisted that she stay at the estate instead of a hotel.

"Ilsa and I have talked. I've told her my intentions of making Savannah my heir."

He waved his arm to encompass the vast lands that could be seen from the balcony. "Everything you see here, the house, the estate, the vineyards, and all the property within I'm leaving to our daughter."

"*My* daughter." Dina rubbed her arms to ward off the chill in the air.

"What did you expect? I want the best for her."

"She might not be yours."

"That's cruel. I choose to believe she is."

Dina took a moment to consider her next words. "That's very generous. How did Ilsa react?"

"She completely understands."

"You didn't tell her about—?"

"Of course not," Malcolm said. "No reason to hurt her. I know this will be a lot for Savannah to accept, and she has no experience in the vineyards. I could hardly bring her here while Da was alive. But she's here now, and she seems eager to learn. My idea was to arrange a marriage between Savannah and the son of the family who owns the next vineyard, Lukas Baeder, to keep her close."

"Yes, Savannah filled me in, but an arranged marriage? That's not done anymore. Today, people fall in love."

"Like we did?"

"We were not in love," Dina objected.

"That's not how I remember it." For a moment it seemed to Dina that Malcolm was about to take her into his arms. And she yearned for that. She needed to limit the time she spent around her ex-brother-in-law. "And I had planned for Savannah to take over my business."

"Did you ever ask her what she wanted?"

"Well, no." Dina chewed her bottom lip. "I told Savannah about us."

Malcolm's eyes widened. "She knows she's my daughter?"

"She knows she might be. But Ilsa and Connor must never know. She thinks of Connor as her father. I don't want to take that away from her."

"I understand. Since Da died, Connor and I have grown close again." I'm truly sorry, Dina. About everything. If things had been different, you and Savannah would have been mine."

"I know, but you have a wonderful life here and a wonderful partner in Ilsa."

"And you?"

"I have Savannah and my business."

"But no one special to warm your bed?"

Dina wiped away a tear. "On occasion. When it needs warming."

"And does it need warming right now?" Malcolm said, toying with her bow and bringing his hand down to cup her face. His lips gently touched hers, and she quivered but soon got herself under control.

"You haven't changed a bit, Mal. I think I dodged a bullet when your father interrupted us that night."

"What do you mean?"

"I have hoped Ilsa and Connor would never find out about us. But I have some conditions."

Malcolm's eyebrows narrowed. "After all this time? And what would those be?"

****

"Savannah, does Andreas still want that land of your uncle's?"

"Yes, most definitely, Mom. We have a small model garden, but he has much bigger plans. He needs that land."

"Well, I've had a talk with Malcolm, and we've come to an agreement. Malcolm is going to give you that land as a wedding gift."

"Andreas is fully prepared to pay a fair price for it."

"That won't be necessary. Tell him to keep his money. He can't afford it, anyway."

"How did you get him to change his mind?"

"I threatened to tell Connor about that night I left him, and I might have implied I'd do the same with Ilsa."

"Mother, that's blackmail."

"That's right. I'm not above that. Your uncle ruined my life, and it's about time he paid for it."

"But you said you hated Scotland and couldn't wait to get away."

"That was only an excuse. I could have been happy there. I would have been happy. I loved your father—still do."

"You still love my da?"

"Of course."

"What about Uncle Malcolm?"

"Mal is the sort of man that turns a woman's head, stirs her passion. I was susceptible to his charms. He does it because he can. To him, it's a game. It's not the sort of feeling that lasts. Once he had me, he'd be on to the next woman."

"Sort of like it is with Lukas."

"Yes," Dina agreed. "They are alike in many ways. Hard to resist but not the kind of men you can count on."

"Like Andreas."

"Yes, like your Andreas."

"If you truly loved Da, why didn't you tell him, all those years ago?"

"What good would it have done? Your grandfather wouldn't have allowed it. And I couldn't trust Mal. He would only stir up feelings. And now your father is married."

"So you both stayed alone your whole lives. It seems like such a waste."

"I agree. That's why I want you to be happy. I think you've found the real thing with Andreas. That man is truly in love with you. It's written all over his face every time he looks at you. He adores you."

"And I feel the same way about him."

"That's all I can ask. Your uncle told me he's naming you in his will. When he and Ilsa are gone, he's leaving you the entire vineyard so your Andreas can grow saffron to his heart's content."

"I have to speak to Andreas, but he'll be very pleased. I'll have to tell him the truth. But that's very generous of Uncle Malcolm."

"He owes you—and me—that much."

"Have you been able to find out if he was the one who had Andreas attacked in front of his house?"

"He promises he had nothing to do with it. He did mention there was someone else who wanted Andreas out of town, but he didn't name names. I think it had something to do with a girl named Abby."

"Abby? Did he mean Melk Abbey?"

"I don't know. What's that all about?"

"I'm not exactly sure, but the police don't have any answers, either. We may never know who attacked him."

"How is he doing?"

"He's pretty much recovered. He's so excited about the saffron farm he hardly thinks about the attack."

"You haven't been back to the estate. Malcolm is wondering if everything is okay between you two."

"Well, you told him I know about the two of you, didn't you? What else would he expect?"

"Yes."

"Well, I think what he did was wrong. He changed all of our lives, pulled our family apart. But it was so long ago. No matter what, he will never really be my father."

"I think he knows that."

"I don't want Da to get hurt. I feel uncomfortable around Uncle Malcolm now that I know."

"So am I. I half expect him to steal into my

bedroom at night, right under Ilsa's nose."

"He wouldn't."

"You don't know your Uncle Malcolm. He most definitely would, if he thought he could get away with it."

"Then why are you still there under his roof?"

"Because Ilsa would suspect if I just left."

Chapter Twenty-One

Saffron Fact: A recipe for swan from Le Viandier de Taillevent, a recipe book written by the French king's cook and published in 1300: Skin the bird, then cook it on a spit. Once the bird is on the fire, you must "glaze it with saffron; and when it is cooked, it should be redressed in its skin, with the neck either straight or flat. Endorse the feathers and head with a paste made of egg yolks mixed with saffron and honey."

"Andreas, this is a charming restaurant. But can you afford it?"

Andreas smiled. "Only the best for you. We can splurge once in a while. It just opened. Let's sit outside. It's a lovely night, and we have a beautiful view of the Danube."

"How did you find out about it?"

Andreas shrugged. "That's not important."

The server took their drink order and handed them menus.

"Look at these dishes. It says almost everything on the menu is saffron-infused."

"That's right," explained the server. "We offer authentic Austrian cuisine with a saffron-driven menu that showcases local farmers from soup to the saffron-infused Esterhazy Tarte. "We're committed to serving fresh, locally procured produce. All the dishes prepared in the kitchen are made with locally grown seasonal ingredients."

"Everything sounds delicious. I don't know where to start."

"I thought we'd try the Chef's Table. Chef will make you a sample of a variety of the dishes. You can tell us which ones you like best."

"But that's the most expensive choice on the menu."

"I can afford it. Besides, we're celebrating."

"What are we celebrating?"

"Our first saffron crop, of course."

Andreas tilted his head and looked at Savannah. "I think your bow is on crooked."

Savannah felt her hair. "I'd better check it in the ladies' room. I'll be right back."

When Savannah returned, Andreas was on one knee.

"Andreas, are you okay?"

"I will be." He reached for her hand. "Savannah Sutherland, will you marry me?"

"Andreas! You already asked and I already said yes."

"But I didn't have the ring. Now I do."

Andreas handed her a box.

She opened it solemnly. And she was speechless.

"Is that a yes?"

"Yes!" she screamed.

He placed the ring on her finger. It was a perfect fit. "Now help me up. I'm still stiff from the attack."

Andreas walked with a slight limp the doctors feared would plague him for the rest of his life. It didn't make him any less dear in her eyes. In fact, it gave him a vulnerability she found appealing, even sexy.

Savannah helped him into his chair.

"Andreas, my God! This ring is beautiful. And it's huge. How can you afford this?"

"It's a family heirloom. You thought you were marrying a poor saffron farmer. The truth is my family has money. I don't like to talk about it."

"I'm not marrying you for your money."

"I know that."

"When did you get it? We've been together since you were in the hospital."

"I had my mother send it."

"It must be—"

"The center stone is five carats."

Savannah couldn't stop looking at the ring.

"I love it. Oh, I can't wait to show it to my mother."

"Maybe she'll feel better about us. Maybe your Uncle Malcolm won't be so anxious to chase me out of town if he realizes I can support you."

"I forgot to tell you. Mother said Uncle Malcolm is leaving me his entire estate, the winery, everything."

"That's wonderful. Now I don't have to go begging for land."

The chef came over and shook hands with Andreas.

"And this must be your beautiful bride-to-be. Andreas, she's even more lovely than you described. You picked her up in a train station?"

"You two know each other and you know the story of how we met?" Savannah asked.

"The guy can't stop talking about you to anyone who will listen. It gives something to talk about other than saffron. What do you see in him anyway?"

"That's enough, Max, I saw her first, and she's already said yes."

"Some guys get all the luck."

"Savannah Sutherland, meet Maximilian Renner."

"So you're the Max in Maximilian's?"

"The one and only. My man here is the silent partner."

"Silent partner?" Savannah turned to Andreas. "What is he talking about?"

Andreas's eyes twinkled. "I'm part owner."

"Part owner?"

"Remember I told you I wanted to partner with a restaurant to serve saffron dishes from local producers?"

"But I had no idea you wanted to own the restaurant."

"Max is from Vienna. We were at university together. He was all the rage in New York. I talked him into coming back and opening this place. He can take advantage of the busy riverboat trade. The boats dock right down the street."

"Y-you own the restaurant?"

"Yes, but I only supply the money and the saffron."

"All the saffron comes from our little garden?"

"Yes, but Max is the true genius behind the venture."

"Andreas is being modest. It helps if you're a Habsburg."

"Andreas, you never told me that. Is that true?"

"Yes, he's Austrian nobility, heir apparent of the House of Habsburg, even though it was abolished in 1919, but he's still part of Austrian society. And speaking of houses, have you been to his home in

Vienna?"

"Not yet. Andreas has spent most of his time recuperating."

"Your future husband lives in a Viennese palace. An actual *schloss*, with a royal ballroom, built between 1713 and 1719 by Johann Lukas von Hildebrandt. There's even a moat, and he has a family crest, although it's defunct. You're marrying into Austrian royalty, you know," said Max, "even if they're no longer in power. You're going to have a title."

"A title?"

"Yes, didn't Andreas mention it? He is Count von something or other."

"Andreas, why didn't you tell me?"

Andreas frowned. "Maybe for the same reason you didn't tell me Signature Accessories was more than just a stand-alone bow store in Charleston."

Savannah's face reddened. "How did you know?"

"A little thing called the Internet. I Googled Signature Accessories out of curiosity. And there was your mother's net worth spread out for all the world to see. No matter. I wanted to maintain an aura of mystery. Max, don't you have somewhere to be? We all have our secrets. Get back in the kitchen before you reveal all of mine."

"You haven't met the Countess?"

"The Countess?"

"Andreas's mother."

"Not yet. Will I have to bow to her or curtsy?"

"Nothing like that," Andreas assured.

"I'm surprised she didn't move into the hospital," said Max.

"I didn't tell her about the attack," Andreas said.

"Andreas just looks like a destitute professor, when actually he's a world-renowned botanist. He hides his brilliance behind his farmer's overalls."

"Saffron farmers don't wear suits," Andreas reasoned. "Are you trying to put her off me?"

"Just the opposite. Miss Sutherland, I love your bow."

"What is it with boys and bows?"

"Don't answer that, Max," Andreas said. "I don't think I should let you out of the house wearing those bows anymore. From now on, you wear the bows only for me. In fact, wear only the bow and nothing else."

"Andreas!"

"Max, we'll have the Chef's Table."

"I have to say, people are loving the saffron-infused dishes," said Max. "They're asking where they can buy some saffron, and of course I'm directing them to your farm shop."

"Thank you."

"Savannah, it's a pleasure to meet you. If you change your mind about Andreas, I'll be in the kitchen." He kissed her hand and walked away.

"I can't concentrate on anything else when I see you in a bow. I just want to take you home and ravish you."

Savannah laughed, then put her hand out and admired her ring.

"Andreas, I can't wait to marry you. But won't your family expect you to marry a European princess?"

"You are my princess. I couldn't find a more perfect match. I feel like a king when I'm with you. My family will love you. I literally can't wait to make you my wife. I'm so glad you suggested moving the wedding up."

"Me too, I—"

"You said your mother needs to get back to the States."

"Yes and I—well, yes."

"Is there something you're not telling me?"

"No, I…mean I—" Savannah's hands rested on her stomach. "A girl has to maintain an aura of mystery."

"You know you can tell me anything."

Savannah paused. "I recently found out that, well, I, I don't know who my father is."

"What?"

"Well, I always thought it was Connor Sutherland, but after talking to my mother, it might be Uncle Malcolm."

"There's no way you could be Malcolm Sutherland's daughter."

"I might be. Regardless, my uncle doesn't have any children. He thinks of me as a daughter. That's why he's leaving me his vineyard."

"Well, I don't care who your father is. I love you and I want to spend the rest of my life with you." Andreas reached across the table and took Savannah's hand. "Savannah Sutherland, soon to be Bauer, Max is right. I don't know why you agreed to marry me. I don't know how I got so lucky. But I'm going to spend my life making sure you don't regret it. We have a whole lifetime to learn about each other."

Chapter Twenty-Two

Saffron Fact: Saffron is sometimes called the red gold.

Andreas straightened his silk tie and smoothed the smartly-tailored jacket of his bespoke business suit. He'd traded in his blue jeans for more respectable garb. He wanted to make a statement and leave an impression. He needed to be taken seriously. He was responsible for someone else now.

"I'm here to see the Reverend Father."

"Do you have an appointment?"

"No, but he'll see me."

"What did you say your name is?"

"Bauer, Andreas Bauer."

The clerk picked up the phone and repeated the request.

"The Reverend Father will see you now."

Andreas walked in, and Father Abbott indicated a chair on the other side of his desk.

"I thought we'd seen the last of you," said the Abbott.

"I'm afraid your thugs botched the job. They didn't manage to kill me. But they nearly succeeded."

"I don't know what you're talking about."

"Sure you do. I know it was you who ordered them to beat me to a pulp."

"Now why would I do that?"

"Because I'm the last link to your secret. A secret that could destroy the Abbey."

"Why should I be concerned? You have no proof."

"So you admit you did try to have me silenced."

"So what if I did. Why are you here?"

"I'm here to inform you that I have a copy of both of your saffron manuals."

"How did you get a copy?"

"I hand copied the manuals, but I also used my cell phone."

"That's not allowed."

"I didn't use a flash."

The Reverend Father frowned.

"And should anything happen to me, I have left with my lawyer a copy of the manuals and a letter explaining how the Abbey stole the English ransom payment. You may think me a simple saffron farmer, but you should know I'm related to the Countess Karoline, the last of the Habsburg dynasty."

"That's impossible."

"It's true, and I've discussed this with my father. I'm sure you are aware that the Habsburgs have connections throughout Europe. I know you wouldn't want to find yourself banished to a remote abbey in some third-world country. I could make that happen, and I'd love to do it. You would sorely miss all of the luxuries and pleasures to which you've become accustomed."

The Reverend Father glared at Andreas.

"Then again, I've been toying with the idea of publishing some of my research in a journal article on the subject, which I imagine would have repercussions beyond the scientific community and might even find its way to the major news outlets. It would perhaps be of interest to the monastic world.

"Or I could take your secret to my grave. You could continue with your plush arrangement here at Melk Abbey, leering at your Klimts and whatever else goes on around here. And I could go on living without fear of anything happening to me or my loved ones. It's your choice."

"How do I know I can trust you?"

"You'll just have to take my word on faith. That's a concept you should be intimately familiar with. I know I can't trust you, which is why I had to put some safeguards in place."

Andreas rose. "That should conclude our business. I hope I have the pleasure of never seeing you again. I'll show myself out."

Chapter Twenty-Three

Scotland

Saffron Fact: According to Hindu religion, Lord Krishna used to put a mark of saffron on his forehead daily.

Savannah ran toward her father. Connor scooped her up in his arms and hugged her.

"Da," she gulped, trying to hold back the tears, hugging him tight. Connor Sutherland was her father in every way. She'd studied Uncle Malcolm intently after her mother's shocking confession. Of course he *looked* just like her father. They were identical twins, after all.

But the two men were as different as the sun and the moon. Uncle Mal was a glad hander. Always the center of attention. Great man to have at a party. But Da—Da was a constant, cool and competent, preferring the shadow to the spotlight. He was a man you could count on. To hold her when she scraped her knee and sing to her when she was sick or rock her to sleep when she was having a bad dream. She was just getting to know Uncle Mal, but Da was her North Star, the one she'd run to when Dina was, well, being Dina.

To be honest, Dina and Uncle Malcolm were better suited for each other. She squeezed Connor tighter, wanting never to let him go.

"I missed you, lass. We were so worried about you. What are those tears?"

"It's just that I haven't seen you in so long. I missed my Da. How was the honeymoon?"

"It was great. It feels good to be with someone. And you, my little girl, are getting married. I go away for a few weeks, and look what happens. Is he good enough for you?"

"He's wonderful."

"Isn't it a bit sudden?"

"Yes, but I love him."

"Mal says he's a saffron farmer. Where did you find him? On FarmersOnly.com?"

"How do you know about that site?"

"Your new stepmother knows a lot of things. Turns out you *can* teach an old dog new tricks."

"Da!" Savannah shook her head. Sometimes her Da was worse than her mother. He was loosening up, courtesy of his new wife.

"We didn't meet on FarmersOnly.com. We met at the St. Valentin's train station. It was very romantic. It's true. He is a farmer, but so much more."

"Do I have to have a talk with the lad?"

"No, Da. You'll scare him off. Mother already had a talk with him, and he's still here."

"Well, then, he's a keeper. I'll look forward to meeting him. Where is he now?"

"I think he went to a falconry demonstration. Afterward, he and his dad are going to play golf. His mother and sisters are on a Glenturret Distillery tour and a whisky tasting. Then they're going to drive through the Trossachs National Park. We'll all meet for dinner."

"Well, I need to show them around Glen Castle Inn. I hope they're enjoying the property."

"How could they not?"

"I made sure they got the best rooms, and I've booked the honeymoon suite for you and Andreas. I put your mother in a room on the top floor."

"The tiny one they call the garret, the one that has no elevator?"

"That's the one."

"She'll hate it."

"I know." Connor smiled.

"I can't wait for you to meet Andreas. He's really looking forward to meeting you. He's already survived Hurricane Dina, and he still wants to marry me, so you're going to show well. I haven't met Andreas's family yet. I'm a little nervous. They're royalty."

****

"Savannah dear, it's so wonderful to finally meet the woman who stole my son's heart. From the moment he met you, he hasn't stopped talking about you. It's a welcome change from saffron."

Savannah laughed. "He can go on about saffron."

The countess gathered her close for a hug. She was a lovely woman, petite with ash blonde hair and blue eyes, dressed in a fashionable blue suit. She didn't wear a crown but she had a royal air about her.

"Welcome to the family. Thank you for taking such good care of Andreas in the hospital. I still can't believe he never told me about the attack."

"Well, for the first few days he was in a coma. When he regained consciousness, he didn't want to worry you." Savannah flashed her ring. "Thank you for the ring. It's magnificent."

160

The countess lifted Savannah's hand. "It looks like it was made for you. Andreas raved about your beauty, but he didn't do you justice. And that bow you're wearing is lovely. So unique."

"My mother manufactures them. I'll ask her to create one for you."

"At my age?"

"My mother still wears them. I'm her walking catalogue. She's made one to match my wedding dress. Bridal wear is one of her most profitable lines."

Andreas's sisters came into the room and hugged her in turn.

"I'm Elisabeth. We're so thrilled to finally meet you. You've made our brother very happy. He's finally started talking about something other than saffron."

"And I'm Maria. I never thought he'd find anyone. He always has his nose in a book or his hands in the dirt. We can't wait until you become our sister."

"Did he tell you how we met?"

"At a train station. St. Valentin's, of all places."

"Yes, isn't that romantic?"

"I never thought of my brother as the romantic type, but there's still hope."

Maria pointed to Savannah's bow. "I love this. I have to have one. And I love the Inn. This is such a lovely property."

"Yes, I grew up here…well, I spent my summers here with my da. It was always my dream to get married here. I can't wait for you to meet my father and mother."

Marilyn Baron

Part Three
The Wedding

Marilyn Baron

Chapter Twenty-Four
Dina

History is repeating itself. It wasn't that many years ago that I walked down this same aisle with Connor Sutherland. We were so happy then. And in love. We had our whole lives ahead of us. What happened? I'm single, and Connor has lost his mind over a vacuous, bosomy waitress—Brandi, or Bambi, or Kiki, or something like that. Look at her. Her cleavage is overflowing that tasteless off-the-rack dress she's wearing, giving her new husband and all of the other men in the room an eyeful. Didn't anyone ever teach her that less is more? A simple, tasteful bow would have drawn more attention than all the low-cut dresses in the world.

I see my ex-husband stealing a glance at me, chic and still slim in my Paris creation and my magnificent diamond-and-lace bow. Eat your heart out, Connor Sutherland!

And then I think, who would I be if I hadn't slept with Connor's brother? Would I have started Southern Signature Accessories? If Ian hadn't banished Mal, he never would have gone to Dürnstein and Savannah might never have met Andreas. Everything happens for a reason. As hard-bitten as I am, I still believe in fate. Those two were destined to meet. If not in a train station, then somewhere. Things have a way of working out. But where's my happy ending?

And Malcolm, who has a perfectly fine wife. I like Ilsa, I really do, but he can't keep his eyes off me. I do look spectacular. And I'm getting quite a few second looks from some fine-looking Scotsmen. Too bad I'm leaving in the morning.

I did have some civil words with Connor before the ceremony.

"I'm sorry you had to come back to Scotland in the winter. I know how you hate the cold." Connor never could pull off sarcasm. He was too nice.

"True. But I couldn't miss my daughter's wedding. Thank you for hosting us here. The Inn has done a wonderful job. Everything looks perfect. And, congratulations, by the way, on your marriage to—" I can never remember that damn woman's name.

"Cindi."

"Yes, she's quite a young woman." Emphasis on the young, but that barb went right over Connor's thick head.

What I didn't say but wanted to was, "She's young enough to be your daughter. You should be embarrassed."

"It's nice to have someone to share your life with."

Translation: You left me. What did you expect?

I couldn't believe it when I stopped by the old Sutherland home and Connor and Bambi were still living there, probably sleeping in our old bedroom. From the satisfied look on Connor's face, I doubt they are getting much sleep. Luckily, he has no idea what went on in there. Malcolm was right. I never would have been content here. It's like time stood still. I left and no one moved on. Had I stayed, Savannah's story might be entirely different. Certainly mine would be. I hope my daughter's marriage turns out better than mine.

But as I look at Connor, dear Connor, I realize that if he would take me back, I wouldn't hesitate to go to him. I still love him. And, Cindi aside, I believe he still loves me. I would give up my business for him. I would brave the cold of Scotland if we could be together again. But that ship has sailed. I have lived a life of regret. But Cindi isn't going away, not from the way she's clinging to him. She may as well be wearing a flashing neon sign that reads, "Stay away from him. He's mine." She's staked her claim. I had my chance and I blew it.

Chapter Twenty-Five
Malcolm

My daughter is a vision, floating down the aisle with such regal bearing to meet her groom. She reminds me of her mother all those years ago. I still remember the ache of wishing things could be different as I watched that magnificent woman glide into my brother's waiting arms and his bed. Connor didn't know what a gem he had in Dina. I had to wait more than a year to have her. And then my whole world changed. I was cut off from my family until Da passed away. But now I have a good relationship with my brother. It's all based on a lie, but Connor is never going to hear the secret from me.

I can't believe Connor and his trophy wife sleep in the same bed as he had when he was a boy. As he had when he was married to Dina. The same bed where Dina and I experienced our one night of passion. When I stopped by that bedroom earlier this afternoon, all the memories came flooding back.

I walk over to Dina. "You look lovely," I say.

"Thank you."

"Savannah is a vision. You must be very proud."

"I am. You can be too."

That is as close an admission of my paternity as I am ever going to get. Dina as much as confirmed it.

I wipe a tear from my eye. "Thank you for that."

I can't legally claim her, but I'll always know she's mine, in my heart. I can't walk her down the aisle, that's Connor's privilege, but I'm back in her life, and if she accepts my offer, she will remain in Dürnstein. I suppose I should be grateful for that. And for the fact that Saffron Boy turned out to be a royal. I hope he's good enough for my daughter. How different would my life be if I hadn't slept with my brother's wife? Back in Scotland and definitely not running the winery.

Dina was speaking again. "Now, I expect you to be civil to Andreas. And come through on your promises."

"You can count on it. Now that he's my son-in-law—my nephew. Turns out we have a lot in common. Saffron Boy has a pretty good working knowledge of vineyards."

"Don't let Savannah hear you call him that."

"Of course not. But I'm leaving the estate in good hands. What about you? What are you going to do when you return to Charleston?"

"Run my business like I always do."

"I hope that keeps you warm at night."

"Bastard," she whispers. "Maybe not, but it's always dependable."

Ilsa comes up to me just then and grabs my arm proprietarily. "Don't you just love weddings?"

"Yes, darling." I tighten my grip on Ilsa. *From now on I am going to be worthy of you in thought and in deed,* I promise silently. I already ruined my brother's life and disappointed my father. I've visited my father's grave and apologized for my bad behavior at the cemetery. I'm grateful for a second chance.

"And Dina, Savannah looked like a princess walking down that aisle."

"She did look lovely," Dina agrees, adding, "Ilsa, I love that dress. You must let me make you a bow to go with that."

"Imagine me in a bow. Aren't I too old to wear a bow?"

"Nonsense. No one is too old for a bow."

Dina flashes a knowing look at me as if she knows I am already imagining it.

"Men and their lust," Dina says. "Most people think bows are for women. But they're really for men. I know what men want. Which is why my business is so successful."

Chapter Twenty-Six
Ilsa

You certainly have the market cornered on lust, Dina. Ever since you entered our home, I can almost smell it on you and on my husband. You don't have to be a maths expert to do the addition. One and one is two. Dina and Malcolm, the perfect pair. Answer to that thorny question I haven't wanted to face, solved. You've been dancing around each other since you arrived in Dürnstein. There's something between you. And you think you're hiding it.

I remember the first time I laid eyes on Malcolm Sutherland. His father dragged him to the vineyard by the scruff of his neck, like a sheep farmer dragging a lamb to the slaughter. Something was off about that whole affair.

Papa and Ian Sutherland had known each other during the war. They had a bond but wouldn't talk about it. Strange bedfellows. A Scotsman and an Austrian. On opposite sides of the conflict. Ian dropped his son off like a hot potato. The mad was steaming off him like a fresh-brewed cup of coffee. He huddled with Papa in the study with great intensity, and then he was gone, never to return except for our wedding, which he dutifully performed like a character in a charade. And Malcolm never went home to Scotland, not for Christmas or any other holiday. Didn't he miss his brother, his twin? Why would he cut himself off from his family?

I was much younger than he, just a slip of a girl, but old enough to notice him working in the vineyard, picking grapes, powerful, shirtless, sweat pouring off his body in the summer, and always the first to volunteer to rise early to pick the grapes for ice wine in the winter. How many times did I go to bed dreaming of that body covering mine?

Papa respected him, trained him, treated him like a son. After years of watching him, yearning for him, I was finally grown up enough to hatch my plan. I would show up whenever he was around, in my tightest dresses, accidentally letting a sleeve drop to reveal a hint of breast. Or I'd press a cold bottle of water against my chest, trying to give him the best come-hither look like the stars in the movies.

For a while he ignored me like a pesky gnat he tried to swat away, or he'd laugh at my antics as if he could see right through me. After months of trying to get the man's attention, I finally marched right up to him and kissed him full on the lips. He pushed me away like he was scalded.

"Don't you ever let your da see you doing that, you little fool," he said. "I'd be out of here so fast. I like it here. I have nowhere else to go."

"Malcolm Sutherland, what will it take to get you to notice me?"

He unleashed a booming laugh. "Oh, I've noticed you all right. How could I not, the way you prance about half naked, coming on to me?"

I was seething mad. He was just the hired help and he was dismissing me. I started to stomp off, but he grabbed me and pulled me close.

"Now, if you want to get noticed by a man, you have to kiss like you mean it." And before I could catch my breath, he had me off my feet and was kissing me until I saw stars and almost fainted dead away. I'd never been kissed like that, or ever been kissed before, and I wanted more.

"Malcolm," I sighed, melting in his arms. I wanted him to do that again and again.

He caught me before I fell. "Christ, lass, of course I noticed you. But you're off limits. I'm the worst kind of man. You should stay as far away from me as you can. I'm poison."

But from that moment on, Malcolm Sutherland was it for me. And I arranged to put myself in his path every chance I got. Finally, he couldn't resist me and we were kissing and petting at every opportunity, taking it to the limit. He showed me how to please a man, what he liked, and in return, made me burn for him. I wanted more.

"Lass, you don't know what you're doing to me. If I touch you again I won't be able to stop. I can't control myself around you. You're playing with fire."

Malcolm Sutherland was dangerous and sexy and I was head over heels in love with the man. I mounted a campaign to get Papa's approval for us to be together. I had made up my mind I was going to marry Malcolm Sutherland. And eventually I did.

Mal turned out to be everything a husband should be, the perfect lover, considerate and grateful for all that I and my family offered him. And he repaid my father in full. He made improvements in the vineyard and proved to be a capable manager. I really think I made him happy. I gave him a family, but my biggest regret and heartbreak was that I couldn't give him children, something we both wanted desperately. We had everything to give a child and no one to share it with.

We were close, but Mal never told me what had happened with his family, why he had come to Austria, why he could never go home. When I found out he had an identical twin brother, I couldn't believe he would want to remain estranged. I was an only child and had always wanted a brother or a sister. He did start going back to Scotland after his father died, and he got reacquainted with his brother and his brother's child.

So when Mal invited Savannah to come for the summer to learn the wine business and talked to me about his desire to leave her the winery, I was ecstatic. Savannah would be the child we never had. The child I could never give him. Or that he could never give me. Or that we couldn't give each other. All I knew was that Mal's eyes lit up whenever she was around so I welcomed her into our house like she was my very own.

Then Dina showed up. The way she looked at my husband and he at her, I knew she was at the heart of the family problem. And the way Mal looked at Savannah, like she was his pride and joy, didn't add up. Dina was the common denominator. She had left her husband at the very same time his brother came to the winery. Exactly what it was they were hiding I didn't know and I didn't want to know. Not that anything happened under my roof. I trusted my husband. It was Dina I didn't trust. I was happy when she moved her perfect body into a hotel and took her bow collection with her. But then Malcolm insisted she return to the estate. She was family, after all. What could I say?

One side benefit was that Malcolm suddenly became more amorous after Dina showed up. She'd unleashed the lust in him. Like any man, he had his needs. He was very physical, and since he couldn't have Dina, he took me every chance he got. I'm not complaining, mind you. In that way, she has been good for our marriage. Her presence reignited the spark we once had. I am determined to keep him satisfied. But Dina is a powder keg waiting to explode, and I don't want my marriage to be a casualty.

Chapter Twenty-Seven
Cindi

That stuck-up cow is sucking all the air out of the room. Who does she think she is, the Queen of England? My God, the woman is in her mid-forties and she's still wearing those bloody bows. Still flirting with all the men in the room like she was a teenager.

Well, fight fire with fire, I always say. I adjust my dress so more of my "assets" are on display. Connor is practically salivating at the sight of them. Well, I have a surprise waiting at home for my new husband. A woman like Dina Sutherland (she still kept her married name and that sticks in my craw) isn't woman enough to keep him. The skinny bitch. I'm not going to make that mistake. I'm all about pleasing my handsome new husband. Old school, I know. But as soon as I found myself in the family way, and the father, a guest at the hotel, long gone, I homed in on Connor Sutherland. I asked around, and the girls all said he'd been pining away for his ex-wife for more than twenty years. I saw the way he looked at me with hunger in his eyes. But he had no idea of how to go about it. So I helped him along a little.

He is a good man. He will make a good da for my baby. And no one will be the wiser. I was able to quit the damn waitress job at the Inn and get off my swollen feet. A man like Connor will wait on me hand and foot;

rub my feet, even, if I ask him. As the mother of the manager's baby, it wouldn't do to have me work. He will be so happy when I tell him about the new addition to the family. I'm planning a special celebration for just the two of us tonight.

He'd never say it, but I know he compares me with his ex. And I know I come up short. Her Highness would never get knocked up with another man's baby. She was too smart, too much of a lady.

And as soon as my baby comes, we'll have to move out of that old house and up, of course, to a more respectable neighborhood. Something more worthy of a Sutherland heir. Hasn't the man ever heard of upgrades? Although there isn't much money that I know of, I am beginning to show, and Connor was in the right place at the right time. He hasn't noticed yet that my figure is getting fuller. I put myself out there, to get him, but I acted appropriately shy and inexperienced. He was so lonely and hungry it wasn't much of a struggle. I teased him mercilessly until I finally, reluctantly, let him have his way with me. And then, good girl that I am, I insisted he make an honest woman of me. I barely had time to seal the deal and convince him he couldn't live without me and that I couldn't wait to be with him. So, the sudden wedding and extended honeymoon. Men are so thick. But Connor is sweet, and I will try my best to make him happy.

Now, Connor's twin brother, Malcolm—there is a man. I tried my darnedest to proposition him at the rehearsal dinner. But he wasn't having any of it. I let him look his fill, and I could tell he was interested, but his possessive wife was always hovering about.

And I can't wait to rub Dina's nose in my fertility. The dried-up old witch. She couldn't hold on to a man. And I can't wait for Connor's daughter to go back to Austria. She's such a Daddy's girl. Well, maybe I'll have a daughter, and then Savannah will be out of sight and out of mind.

Chapter Twenty-Eight
Connor

My God. It's been so long since I've seen her, and she hasn't changed a bit. She's still my beautiful Dina. The same girl who walked down the aisle to me all those years ago. Who swore her forever vows. We were so in love and so happy, and then all of a sudden she was gone, without a word. Some nonsense about Scotland being too cold for her blood. Well, I could have heated up her blood, kept her warm. But she didn't give me a chance. Da tried to tell me I'd find another woman, but I never did, until Cindi.

I was on my way home from work to surprise her for our anniversary. She had planned a special dinner for us. I knew I'd been working long hours, but I was doing it for her, to give us a better life. I only wanted the best for my new bride. And then, Da said, she left on a plane, back to Charleston. She was homesick or unhappy or something. I wish I knew. Da said good riddance, and Malcolm left at the same time.

God, I've been so lonely all these years. Of course the news of Savannah, my daughter, changed everything. I went to Charleston to claim my family, but Dina was having none of it. Da arranged for Savannah to spend summers in Scotland. She was the light of my life. And now our little girl is getting married.

If I could, I'd take Dina back in a minute. I half hoped that her coming here, seeing me, after all this time, would joggle her memory and, by some miracle, she would come back to me.

But somehow, Cindi has come into my life, like a thunderstorm, shaking things up. It was a whirlwind courtship. She was sexy and willing, and I was so damn lonely I couldn't resist her charms. I'm old enough to be her father. I've heard the snickers. But I have to move on.

Dina was sweet when she saw me again, but it's obvious she has no interest in me. She's been staying with Malcolm and Ilsa and seems closer to Mal than she ever was to me.

Now I'm just being sentimental. It's the wedding, of course. Seeing my daughter walk down the aisle, looking like a princess, giving her away, reminds me so much of my feelings for Dina. Wife or no wife, I will always love that woman. I gave her my heart for a lifetime. I wish I could hold on to my daughter a bit longer. But young Andreas seems to be a good man, a good match, and I hope to God he will make her happy.

Chapter Twenty-Nine
Andreas

If I hadn't looked up from my paper on the train as we pulled into the Bahnhof of St. Valentin, I might never have seen her. If I hadn't acted on the urge to get off the train, I might never have met her. If I hadn't looked into her eyes, and she hadn't come over to me, we might never have talked. And we might not be walking down the aisle at this very moment.

I'm a scientist. I never believed in fate or destiny. Savannah is sure it was fate that brought us together. Whether it was fate, a heavenly force, luck, or serendipity, I'm grateful that we met, that we talked on the train, and that we're going to share our lives.

Before I met Savannah I was content. I had a routine. I had my work with saffron.

But now, I can't imagine a life without her. I have met my perfect mate. We will water our garden and see what grows.

She has an open heart, a pure soul, a loving spirit. The fact that she's the most beautiful creature I've ever seen on this earth is a bonus. I don't know why she chose me. But I will be forever grateful.

As her father walks her down the aisle and hands her off to me, he says, half in tears, "Take care of my little girl." I assure him that I will. She is the most priceless gift I could ever receive.

I look at her and whisper, "You look like a princess." She smiles, shyly, and we turn toward the officiant to be united forever.

Chapter Thirty

Saffron Fact:
"Your lips drop sweetness like honeycomb, my bride, syrup and milk are under your tongue, and your dress had the scent of Lebanon. Your cheeks are an orchard of pomegranates, an orchard full of rare fruits, spikenard and saffron, sweet cane and cinnamon."
—*Song of Solomon*

Her wedding was everything Savannah had imagined. A dream come true. She was about to be married at Glen Castle Inn on Loch Lomond. Her father was waiting to walk her down the aisle. Her mother and father would finally be together, if only for the ceremony. She'd half-hoped that when Da saw her mother, after all those years, his heart would open up, and hers, and that they'd come together. Cindi didn't figure into that equation. Cindi made herself scarce, supervising the caterers, and managed to stay as far away from Dina as possible. That was good. It was hard to warm up to that woman. But if she made her Da happy, okay. She was not going to let go of her marriage. She was going to hang on tight to Andreas and make him the happiest man in the world, as happy as he'd made her.

When in earlier years she'd imagined her groom, he had been outfitted in a kilt, with a vest and a dress white shirt, steeped in Scottish tradition. Andreas had offered to wear a kilt. But in the end, he decided to wear a tailored gray tuxedo. And he looked quite handsome. His parents and sisters had flown in from Vienna. Da and Uncle Malcolm were looking fine in their traditional Scottish garb.

Savannah wore a white designer gown—Dina had insisted—and her mother had created a priceless diamond bow in lieu of a tiara—fastened at the top of her head, from which her gauzy-white, pearl-encrusted floor-length veil trailed. But no bow could compare to the ring Andreas had given her. It was worthy of a princess. And she felt like a fairytale princess in the elegant setting. It was truly enchanting.

She and Andreas made their entrance on a seaplane, and the weather cooperated. It was a beautiful but crisp sunny day. With the Highland piper behind her and the ceremonial sword ahead of her, the grand toastmaster announced her arrival.

Following the ceremony, the guests walked along the lake to the cruiser for a one-hour Champagne reception before returning to the hotel for dinner. Andreas was impressed with the hotel, and they took advantage of strolling the grounds, relaxing at the bar with stunning views across Loch Lomond, relaxing at the spa, playing golf, and partaking of all the other leisure activities.

She was most looking forward to the honeymoon, which would start at the resort for a relaxing three-night stay, and then they would fly to the Amalfi Coast for two weeks. Andreas had already made it clear he wanted to start a family right away and she was in agreement. Upon returning from their honeymoon, they would get right back to work.

After a few private words with Dina, soon after Savannah's engagement, Uncle Malcolm had agreed to provide the acreage Andreas needed to farm his saffron in earnest. Andreas had begun by planting 30,000 saffron bulbs and now, thanks to the closed wine terraces on Uncle Malcolm's property, he cultivated around 300,000 saffron crocuses.

Andreas's restaurant venture with Max was successful. His cruise excursion business was booming. His goal was to put Dürnstein on the map for saffron. He mentored other saffron farmers and encouraged them to start farms in the area. He would give the vintners a run for their money, although wine would always be popular in the Wachau.

****

Months after they returned to their own home, night fell, and she and Andreas sat on their rocking chairs holding hands on the porch, gazing out at the railway tracks of their own station, feeling the delicious breeze wafting off the Danube, each thinking their private thoughts.

She thought back to the moment she and Andreas met at the Bahnhof of St. Valentin. She was convinced it was fate. She thanked the stars for her wonderful life and for the twins she was carrying, a boy and a girl. She hadn't told Andreas yet. But she knew he'd be over the moon. Some secrets were worth savoring. Some surprises were worth the wait.

"…The Devil is Loose"

Dürnstein, Austria, was first mentioned in the history books because in 1192, in the castle above the town on the Danube, fifty miles west of Vienna, King Richard I of England was held captive.

On October 9, 1192, Richard the Lionheart, ill with scurvy, left the Holy Land during the Third Crusade and set out for England on a dangerous land route through central Europe. On his way to the territory of his brother-in-law Henry the Lion, Richard was captured shortly before Christmas 1192 near Vienna by the men of Leopold V, Duke of Austria, who accused Richard of arranging the murder of his cousin Conrad of Montferrat (Italy) in Jerusalem.

Richard was passed from stronghold to stronghold in lands controlled by Leopold. On March 28, 1193, Richard was brought to Speyer and the duke finally handed the king over to Henry VI, Holy Roman Emperor, who imprisoned him in Trifels Castle.

Seizing Richard was considered an illegal act, as Pope Celestine III had decreed that knights who took part in the crusade were not to be molested as they traveled to and from the Holy Land. Duke Leopold and Henry VI were subsequently excommunicated for capture and wrongful imprisonment of a fellow crusader.

Finally, on February 4, 1194, Richard was released along with this message, "Look to yourself; the devil is loose."

Acknowledgments

I visited Dürnstein, Austria, on a Danube River cruise and took the road less traveled by. Instead of going on a tour of the local winery, I opted for an excursion to a saffron farm, which is what inspired me to write this book.

The saffron farmer, Bernhard Kaar, an ecologist and botanist, grows top-quality saffron and produces gourmet saffron products following the regional cultivation tradition found in eighteenth-century texts in its historical growing area. His company, Wachauer Safran Manufaktur, is located in front of an old railway station. He actually did meet his wife at the Bahnhof of St. Valentin. But the rest of the story is fiction. The company does sell some amazing products, which you can order at https://www.safranmanufaktur.com/. I took home the saffron honey and the saffron salt and wish I had stocked up on more products.

I also visited the magnificent 900-year-old Melk Abbey, featured prominently in this book, whose famous Baroque library really does house two books about saffron. One of the books, written by the theologian Ulrich Petrak in 1797, is called "Practical Lessons in Growing the Lower Austrian Saffron."

On a Rhine River cruise, I stopped at the town of Speyer, Germany, where King Richard was imprisoned for a period. In fact, the Historical Museum of the Palatinate on the Cathedral Square was hosting an exhibit about Richard the Lionheart while I was there. I also took an excursion to a vinegar estate in that city.

A local winery in Bacharach, in the heart of the Upper Middle Rhine Valley, was the inspiration for the

Kleppinger vineyard. Our cruise began in Basel, Switzerland, stopped in France, Germany, and Holland, and ended in Amsterdam, where I was fortunate enough to see the tulips in bloom at the Keukenhof Gardens. And in Strasbourg, France, I got to taste the delicious Gugelhopf cakes.

The Glenn Castle Inn on Loch Lomand in Scotland was inspired by the real-life Cameron House on Loch Lomond, a popular wedding site and one of the most beautiful properties I've ever visited. If you're ever in Scotland, you should consider staying there. Like Savannah, I was mesmerized by the sight of the lake and stayed up all night just watching it.

Although the facts about King Richard's imprisonment and ransom are not entirely clear, according to the history books, only one ransom is recorded as having been paid for his release. So the payment of a second ransom and the idea of a saffron conspiracy stems entirely from my imagination.

A word about the author…

Marilyn Baron writes in a variety of genres, from women's fiction to historical romantic thrillers and romantic suspense to paranormal/fantasy. She's received writing awards in Single Title, Suspense Romance, Novel with Strong Romantic Elements, and Paranormal/Fantasy Romance, and was the Finalist in the 2017 Georgia Author of the Year Awards (GAYA) in the Romance Category for her novel *Stumble Stones* and the Finalist in the 2018 GAYA Awards in the Romance Category for her novel *The Alibi*. Her new novel, *The Saffron Conspiracy: A Novel*, is her 24th work of fiction. A public relations consultant in Atlanta, she is co-chair of the Roswell Reads Steering Committee and serves on the Atlanta Authors Committee.

To find out more about Marilyn's books, please visit her Web site at:

http://www.marilynbaron.com